PURITAN

By Winston Phelps

HERITAGE BOOKS, INC.

Published 1987 By

HERITAGE BOOKS, INC.
3602 Maureen Lane, Bowie, Maryland 20715
301-464-1159

ISBN 1-55613-077-5

A Catalog Listing Hundreds Of Titles On
History, Americana, and Genealogy
Available Free Upon Request

TABLE OF CONTENTS

Preface   v

Acknowledgements   vii

Introduction   ix

Chapter One - Puritan Immigration and Settlement   1

Chapter Two - Puritan Religion   33

Chapter Three - Indian and European Neighbors   55

Chapter Four - Biographical Sketches   77

Conclusion   89

Index   91

PREFACE

Our Puritan forefathers left a confusing legacy. We can admire their bravery, but deplore their religious bigotry. We can applaud their perseverence in overcoming enormous obstacles as they planted their colonies in the New World, yet feel a sense of shame as we learn how ruthlessly they treated some of the Indians, and, indeed, how ruthlessly they treated their fellow colonists who happened to hold different beliefs.

For some of us the colonial period is fascinating at least partly because it is so unlike anything with which we are familiar. None of our Twentieth Century experiences equip us to appreciate the trials those Seventeenth Century colonists had to accept and the terrors that darkened their lives.

Professional historians know the period well, of course. They have turned out scads of material complete with footnotes, appendices, and bibliographical confirmation. The trouble is, most of these authoritative accounts make for heavy going.

What is offered in this little book is simply a report of happenings, most of them in New England with special attention to the Puritan communities. The people and the events are depicted as their stories have been passed down to us from many sources.

It is possible that those who passed the stories along may have embellished some of the facts. It is even conceivable that the collector who gathered this material may have unwittingly injected a smidgen of embellishment. But the intention has been to give a readable report, an honest report, and a report that doesn't inflict grievous damage to historical accuracy.

Winston Phelps
Spring Hill, Florida
August 1987

ACKNOWLEDGEMENTS

Quotes appearing in this book were taken from the following sources. Page numbers in parantheses indicate where the quotes may be found in the text.

Massachusetts Historical Society paper by Charles Frances Adams, Jr. (14)
The Younger John Winthrop by Robert C. Black III. (34, 37, 38, 49, 60)
Puritanism in the Wilderness by Peter N. Carroll. (3, 5, 19, 20, 49, 61)
The Americans by J. C. Furnas. (16, 41)
The Phelps Family of America, Volumes 1 and 2, by Oliver S. Phelps. (12, 17, 18)
Colonists in Bondage by Abbot Emerson Smith. (11)
Cape Cod by Henry David Thoreau. (2)
A New American History by W. E. Woodward (57, 79)

INTRODUCTION

All of us in our school days learned about Christopher Columbus and his historic voyage in 1492. Then we learned something about the colonies at Jamestown (1607) and Plymouth (1620). But our schooling left a huge gap. We learned little, if anything, about what happened between, say, 1500 and 1607. Here was a span of more than a century. For the average American it became, historically, just a blank page.

In fact, many things of interest happened in that century. We shall trace a few of them to fill in the gap and get something on that blank page.

Once Columbus and the other early explorers had demonstrated that there was a New World over there across the sea, daring projects were launched to exploit the discovery. Greed was one motive, settlement and land ownership was another. Quantities of gold, silver and precious gems were thought to be lying loose upon the ground in the New World, just waiting to be collected. During the 1570's, for example, the Spaniards cut a swath through Mexico, the West Indies and lands to the south, converting, killing and looting as they marched. Shipload after shipload of plunder was sent back to Spain. Some of the ships were hijacked by pirates and others were lost in storms, but quantities of the loot reached Spain and was added to the royal treasury. Other adventurers were itching to get at the New World's bountiful supply of fish and furs. And if this was indeed the Orient, as Columbus believed, there also would be vast riches in silk and spice to be had.

The idea of planting colonies in the New World caught the imagination of leaders in many countries.

In 1526, a Spaniard named Lucas Vasquez de Ayllon settled five hundred men, women and children plus some Negro slaves at the mouth of a river somewhere along the east coast of America. The colony apparently was wiped out by disease. Its precise location has never been determined.

ix

The French under Rene de Laudonniere established a colony in 1564 near the mouth of what is now St. John's River in Florida. Now, Spain considered that part of the world her private domain, so when news of the intrusion reached Madrid, the King of Spain dispatched a naval force to the scene, overpowered the colony, and every soul in that French settlement was murdered. The atrocity was avenged in 1568 with a tit-for-tat response. A French naval force recaptured the site and slaughtered every Spaniard in sight. Life was cheap in those days when sturdy adventurers roamed the world and gloried in combat.

In the 1570's two attempts were made to establish colonies in the Carolinas by the French Huguenots who were fleeing from persecution in their homeland. Their first settlement was wiped out by disease. A second was wiped out by Spanish marauders who overran the settlement, chopped up the Huguenots, and stole everything they could carry off.

The Fisheries

Dreamers in the Sixteenth Century imagined that a stroke of luck would put them on Easy Street once they had found those mythical hoards of gold in the New World. More practical-minded merchants and seafarers put the myths aside and set about exploiting the tangible resources of the sea along the coast of America.

And these resources were vast. Men who had fished the waters around Europe and elsewhere were boggle-eyed when they encountered the fishing grounds off America. Samuel Eliot Morison said there never had been anything to match it:

"No part of the world has ever been so rich in edible fish and other products of the sea as the Newfoundland Banks, the coast of Labrador, and the Gulf of the St. Lawrence."

By the 1570's, scores of fishing vessels from England, France, Spain, Holland, Denmark, and Portugal were sailing regularly across the North Atlantic, loading up with fish from the North American banks, and carrying their cargoes back to Europe.

So great was the activity and so numerous the ships, it nearly created a serious problem of traffic congestion around the banks. When Sir Humphrey Gilbert reached Newfoundland in 1583 he counted thirty-six fishing vessels there: twenty from Spain and Portugal, and sixteen from England and France. Nor does there seem to be any reason to question Sir Humphrey's count. Others at the time have confirmed that large numbers of fishing vessels were regularly engaged in this activity. Some years later, in 1594, the master of the ship *Grace*, a whaler out of Bristol, England, reported that he encountered three-score fishing vessels at Placentia Bay, Newfoundland, and that after rounding Cape Race he counted twenty-two more, all of these English.

Why this extravagant interest in fish? For one thing, the Roman Catholic calendar in the Sixteenth Century had one hundred-sixty fast days; on these days, the eating of meat was forbidden but the eating of fish was okay. For another, poultry and meat were expensive while fish was relatively cheap. Additionally, meat and other foods were difficult to keep for any length of time; reliable methods of refrigeration had not yet been devised. Fish, especially cod, was easily treated by drying and was easy to store. It required no special attention in storage and remained edible over a long period.[1]

Protestant England did not observe the Catholic fast days, of course, so the Church of England had no theological interest in meatless fish days. But the fishing industry was important to England because it employed so many Englishmen. So Parliament, in 1563, with Queen Elizabeth's blessing, passed a law declaring both Wednesday and Saturday to be fish days in Protestant England. This increased the demand for fish and encouraged English fishermen to make the long, risky trip across the North Atlantic to the fishing grounds.

During the fish-drying operation, many of the fishermen built crude huts on the shore near the fishing grounds. They

[1]Some of the fishermen followed a procedure called wet fishing: they simply covered their catch with quantities of salt, then carried the lot back to Europe where the curing process could be completed. Dry fishing was more satisfactory. This procedure required a base on shore where rack tables, called flakes, could be set up. The fish were cleaned, split, lightly salted, then placed on the flakes to dry in the sun. Once thoroughly dried, the salted cod fish required no special attention at all. The fish could be stacked, boxed, or tied in bundles. This made it easy to handle and it would remain a palatable food for months. Cod was the preferred fish for this process because it was a relatively large fish, had firm flesh, and, best of all, was fantastically abundant. It isn't quite true that the fishermen simply anchored on the banks, then collected the cod that leaped onto the deck. But catching cod was almost that easy.

lived in these huts while arranging their fish flakes and tending the fish during the sun-drying process. A few of the fishermen may have stayed ashore on American soil for weeks at a time but there is no evidence that any of them attempted to plant a colony or establish permanent residence.

No one, so far as this writer knows, has ever attempted to guess how many tons of fish were drawn from these fishing grounds in the Sixteenth and Seventeenth Centuries to feed the hungry people of Europe and other parts of the world. Nor has anyone guessed how many tons have been taken in later centuries. Whatever the total, it surely is enormous. Despite fears expressed from time to time that the supply might be depleted, those fishing grounds have continued to provide huge quantities of fish down through the years.

David Ingram's Tales

An interesting character named David Ingram turned up in the London pubs in 1569. Ingram told fascinating tales about his adventures. He was an artful story-teller who mixed fact and fiction so smoothly no listener could be certain whether there might be a grain of truth in his tales or no truth at all. Evenso, he never lacked a rapt audience. Ingram's basic story - quite unproven - was that he had been a British sailor and that he and two other sailors had been put ashore in the fall of 1567 along what is now the shore of the Gulf of Mexico. Why he was put ashore - if he was - never became clear. Maybe he was a troublemaker and the captain dumped him ashore just to get rid of him, rather than stash him in the brig.

Anyhow, Ingram said he started walking north along Indian trails. According to his account, he walked all the way to what is now Maine. The trek occupied him for two years.

Along the way, Ingram told his audience of pub patrons, he came upon many strange sights. There were lambs with red wool. And there were animals as big as horses, but with tusks.

How about gold? Did he find any gold in America? You bet he did! Gold was plentiful, Ingram assured his listeners. In fact it was so plentiful that he often picked up solid gold nuggets as big as his fist. The pub patrons lapped this up.

After his thrilling two-year odyssey in the New World, Ingram said he hailed a French fishing vessel and bummed a ride back to Europe. He seems to have finished out his days as a story-telling pub crawler. But his wild tales may have contributed to the publicity which painted America in a gaudy light. And he may have induced some of the gullible to make the long journey to the American paradise across the ocean where they could collect some of those fist-sized hunks of gold.

Sir Humphrey Gilbert

The notion of colonizing America intrigued Queen Elizabeth of England and an assortment of promoters in the 1570's and 1580's. A great deal was now common knowledge about how to reach America and what might be found when one got there: various explorers - not all of them quite as flaky as David Ingram - had examined the American coast, and hundreds of seamen had crossed the North Atlantic on their way to and from the fishing grounds.

Sir Humphrey Gilbert, a visionary and a man of some standing, came up with an elaborate plan in 1578. The Queen thought his plan was splendid. So she gave him a royal grant, which was the green light he needed to proceed. The royal grant didn't cost the Queen anything.

The next step for Sir Humphrey was to round up some financial backers. He did this by approaching well-to-do Englishmen, showing them the royal grant, feeding them a colorful spiel, then twisting their arms to get them to cough up large wads of cash. In return, Sir Humphrey offered to his patrons generous chunks of the American territory he expected to seize and claim once his project got going.

To a patron named John Dee, Sir Humphrey awarded all the land north of latitude 50 degrees North. (This would encompass most of what is now Canada, plus Alaska and Greenland.) Another patron, George Peckham, received 1,500,000 acres. (This spread included most of what is now Rhode Island and Connecticut, plus parts of a few other states-to-be.) Philip Sidney, a third patron, must have invested an especially large sum in the enterprise. Sir Humphrey awarded him three million acres of America plus two-fifths of all the precious metals and gems to be found in that domain.

Sir Humphrey dreamed up another dandy idea. He decided he would sell some of his land to the English Catholics. This would help rid Protestant England of the pesky Catholics, give the Catholics a place in America where they could have their own colony, and, most importantly, provide Sir Humphrey with a nice additional bundle of funds.

It was, indeed, a proposal with lots of advantages. But Queen Elizabeth turned thumbs down on it. She told Sir Humphrey she would not let the Catholics leave the country until they had paid their fines. (These were fines levied against persons who didn't attend the Protestant church services.) The English Catholics had stoutly refused to attend those services and they were too poor to pay the fines, so their debt climbed higher and higher. It never was paid.

Despite that, Sir Humphrey collected enough money from his patrons to get started. He acquired some ships, organized his crews and set forth bravely with a voluminous set of maps and high hopes.

The first expedition in 1578 was a total bust. The weather was bad, the crews misbehaved and the ships developed leaks. Sir Humphrey's three vessels did not complete the crossing.

Sir Humphrey tried again in 1583. This time he reached Newfoundland where he came upon three dozen fishing vessels busily loading fish for Europe. Sir Humphrey showed the masters of these fishing ships his royal grant signed by the Queen and they accepted his authority with good grace. Thereupon, Sir Humphrey took possession of the entire region for his Queen, and, on 5 August 1583, ordered three laws into effect:

1. Public worship must be in accord with the Church of England.
2. Any move prejudicial to the Queen's "right and possession" will be punished "according to the lawes of England."
3. Anyone uttering words dishonoring Her Majesty was "to loose his ears and have his ship and goods confiscate."

Sir Humphrey must have performed this ritual with impressive flair and confidence – or perhaps the fishermen were interested only in fish and did not care two beans about royal grants, proclamations and such. Anyhow, the fishermen swallowed the procedure hook, line and sinker. They offered no resistance, not even a peep of protest. (The fishermen from Portugal, Spain and other places who did not understand English probably didn't have the foggiest notion what Sir Humphrey was up to, but they went along with it anyhow.)

That marks the peak of Sir Humphrey's grand design. He managed to do some exploring in the Newfoundland area. Then a fierce storm blew in, his ship foundered and he was lost. His elaborate project for establishing colonies in America went down with him, and his patrons who had invested large sums were left holding an empty sack.

Sir Walter Raleigh

Sir Walter Raleigh took up the colonization task in 1584. He, too, approached Queen Elizabeth and was pleased to find her still eager to authorize colonies despite the unhappy record of Sir Humphrey.

The Queen issued a warrant authorizing Sir Walter "to discover search fynde out and viewe such remote heathen and barbarus landes countries and territories not actually possessed by any Christian Prynce."

Unfortunately, Sir Walter had no better luck than Sir Humphrey. His first attempt in 1584 failed, and so did a second attempt four years later.

Sable Island

One partially successful experiment in "colonization" can be recorded in this period. At some undetermined point in the mid-1500's, a Portuguese mariner named Fagundes, while cruising off the North American coast, conceived the idea of settling cattle, horses and pigs on the offshore islands. If the animals survived and flourished, Fagundes reasoned, they would provide meat for him and his crew should they return that way. Other explorers, with the same idea, also may have placed cattle and swine on the islands.

The skimpy record suggests that only one of these programs panned out. Cattle placed on Sable Island, off what is now Nova Scotia, did survive the experience. They multiplied, turned wild, and were available on the island for other mariners who landed there in search of fresh meat.

In 1578 and again in 1584 the French tried to colonize Sable Island with a gang of convicts. On the first attempt, the English got wind of the scheme, charged in with a superior force and routed the French. On the second attempt, a great storm blew in and destroyed the French fleet before the convicts could be put ashore.

Finally, in 1598, the French managed to place sixty convicts on Sable Island. They were left there for five years. At the end of that period, a French mission found eleven of the convict-colonists still alive. They were taken back to France.

Northwest Passage

Meanwhile, repeated efforts were made to find that elusive

Northwest Passage. Even after decades of study and exploration many mariners felt sure there must be some relatively easy way to get through America and on, to the Far East. The pot of gold at the end of this rainbow would be ready access to the silks and spices of the Orient. No one believed America was very wide, and no one seemed to have a realistic idea of the width of the Pacific Ocean. The persistent nagging thought was that one of those larger rivers in the northern part of America must lead to a passage, and that after negotiating that passage the Orient would be within reach.

The widespread ignorance on this basic geography is difficult to understand. After all, Ferdinand Magellan had circumnavigated the globe in 1522. Francis Drake did it in 1579 in the *Golden Hind*. French explorers had moved deep into North America, and Spanish explorers had studied Mexico and what are now the southern reaches of the United States. From the information assembled by these various adventurers one would expect a fairly accurate geographical picture to emerge. But that didn't happen. What emerged was a wildly erroneous picture. Many of the wisest people in the Seventeenth Century felt sure there must be a Northwest Passage.

Moreover, they had no real conception of the distances involved. They seemed to think that if they passed westward from the Atlantic coast they would find the Pacific Ocean's coast at about the longitude of what is now Pittsburgh. And just beyond - possibly about at present-day Des Moine - they would find Japan and China.

So it was that the futile search for the Northwest Passage went on. Martin Frobisher won the backing of the Queen for several voyages, beginning in 1576, in search of the Passage. He failed. John Davis, an experienced explorer, set out with two vessels in 1585 on another search, and again in 1586 with four ships. He also failed.

Ultimately that dream of a Northwest Passage faded away, but while it lasted it was an illusory beacon that fired the hopes of many brave adventurers.

Concluding Remarks

In summing up the record of America in the 1500's, we come away with the conclusion that it was largely a century of failure. The search for gold was a failure. The hunt for a Northwest Passage was a failure. The repeated attempts to establish colonies in the New World were failures.

On the credit side, however, the fur-trading was successful, and the fisheries off the northern shores of America were enormously profitable.

But this testing, probing and exploring in the 1500's, fruitless though much of it appeared to be, was setting the stage for the 1600's when a fresh generation of explorers and colonists would move in and put down permanent roots in America.

CHAPTER ONE

PURITAN IMMIGRATION AND SETTLEMENT

The Great Migration

In scope and in concept the Puritan migration to Massachusetts Bay in the 1630's was unlike anything the world had known. Adventurers had been poking along the coast of America for more than a century – usually taking back to their homelands hair-raising and highly imaginative accounts of their exploits – but none of these early intruders were much interested in colonization; their interests were directed more to adventure, trade, and loot. The Spaniards, lured by the prospect of gold and silver, had systematically invaded and looted native settlements in the West Indies and lower reaches of America. Samuel de Champlain and other French pioneers had pressed deep into present-day Canada and middle America to explore and obtain furs in trade with the Indians.

The English attempted to colonize three sites in America prior to 1630. Sir Walter Raleigh placed a group of colonists on Roanoke Island, off North Carolina, in 1587 but a relief expedition in 1591 found the site abandoned and no trace of any of the colonists. The early settlement at Jamestown (1607) was a disaster. Plymouth (1620) struggled valiantly, but ten years after its founding had a population of only three hundred people.

With this as background, the astonishing success of the Massachusetts Bay settlement becomes even more remarkable. A few Puritans made the crossing in 1629 as sort of an advance guard and established their settlement at what is now Salem, Massachusetts.

It was in the next year, 1630, that the great Puritan migration unfolded. In that year alone seventeen ships carried seventeen hundred colonists into Massachusetts Bay. Included

1

in that fleet was the *Arbella* bearing John Winthrop, leader of the expedition, founder of Boston, and long-time governor of the colony.

By 1643 the population of Massachusetts Bay had soared to sixteen thousand persons. There were now more colonists in settlements such as Lynn, Dorchester, Boston, Ipswich, Salem, Gloucester, and Marblehead (all part of the Massachusetts Bay colony) than there were in all the other American colonies combined. (These towns were under the control of the Massachusetts General Court.)

Meanwhile settlements appeared in other parts of New England, especially in Maine, Rhode Island, and Connecticut. The population of New England reached an estimated one hundred and twenty thousand by 1675.

Deciding to Emigrate

John Winthrop was moved partly by religious zeal and partly by a vision of coming catastrophe when he made his decision to emigrate to America. Winthrop became obsessed by what he regarded as the wave of sinfullness sweeping over England and he was moved to embrace the Puritan cause. He saw decadence all about him, venality in the government, and corruption in the Church of England. And he predicted that all of this depravity surely would lead to disaster. (His vision of disaster was borne out. Only a few years later England was plunged into a bloody civil war.) He moved among his friends, and any others who would listen, warning them of the afflictions falling upon England and inviting them to consider his program for emigration to America. His message was blunt:

England's sinnes, for which the Lord beginnes already to frown upon us, do threaten evil times. Who knows that God hath provided New England to be a refuge for many whome He means to save out of the General Calamity, and seeing the Church hath no place to flie but into the Wilderness, what better work can there be than to goe and provide tabernacle and food for her.

It was a persuasive pitch. Scores of Puritans signed on to accompany Winthrop. Some of them, like Thomas Shepard, were distinguished citizens who had long been saddened by the sinfulness they saw in England:

2

"Our age grows full and proud and wanton. I doe beleeve the Lord is coming to teare and rend from you your choysest blessings of peace and plenty. He will give sore afflictions of famine, war, bloud, mortality, deaths of Gods precious servants especially."

Many of Winthrop's growing band of followers were poor farmers or humble yeomen, but included in the roster was a generous sprinkling of Saltonstalls, Endicotts, and others who, like the educated and wealthy Winthrop, came from well-to-do families and were able to help finance the expedition.

Indeed, one of the unusual features of this great Puritan migration was that it was financed by the migrants themselves. All of the earlier colonial ventures had been financed by London money men who put up the cash, kept a controlling finger on their colonial investment, and fully expected to make a handsome profit on the deal.

Massachusetts Bay was never under the thumb of London bankers. Right from the start, the colonists enjoyed a measure of freedom that was unique in the New World. They were expected to pledge loyalty to the English monarch, but beyond that pledge they were pretty much on their own as they shaped their colony in the wilderness.

Puritan Rebels

The Puritans were rebels. They were rebelling against practices they had seen developing within English society. In their view the established Church of England was departing from its original tenets, indulging in too much pomp and ceremony, getting to be too much like the Church of Rome. Even worse, the Puritans were deeply offended when they found many church leaders soiling their positions by engaging in bribery and graft. The colonists' basic aim was to purify the church – hence the name "Puritan." In the New World they hoped to create their ideal state with its purified faith.

The principal complaint of the Puritans dealt with religious affairs. In the early decades of the Reformation, guidelines for the Protestants were established by John Calvin and widely adopted. The stern, unbending tenets of Calvinism colored most of the Protestant movement for a half century (and, indeed, are still potent guidelines in some Protestant sects today.)

At the turn of the century, however – about 1600 – an anti-Calvinist reaction set in. A learned minority in the Anglican

3

church began to question and reject Calvinist strictures. These questioners gradually found much to admire in the ceremony, the sacramentalism, and the elaborate rites which the Calvinists abhorred.

Bishop William Laud became the outspoken leader of this reaction in England. He not only brought back much of the church ceremony which was so distasteful to many Protestants, he also devised and proclaimed a brand of authoritarianism which was equally repellent. In Laud's view, Kings were established by divine right. Since God could make no error, a King named by God likewise must be free of error. From this line of reasoning, Bishop Laud concluded that anyone who dared to resist or criticize the King was consigned to eternal damnation. This was powerful stuff in a community that took its religion seriously.

Charles I, who became King in 1625, thought Bishop Laud's views were just dandy. It pleased him immensely to be assured that he held power by divine right and to be told that anything he said or did would be errorless. Small wonder that the Bishop buttered up his King and that the King lapped up the adulation. They got along handsomely.

Winthrop and his fellow Puritans couldn't stomach this behavior. They regarded the King as a puppet, Bishop Laud as a tyrant saturated in wrong ideas, and they longed for a return to the strict Calvinism in which they felt most comfortable.

There were other matters that displeased the Puritans. One of these was the Royal practice of granting monopolies. It had long been the custom in England for monarchs to award monopoly rights to friends of the royal family or favored courtesans. As an example, one man might receive the monopoly right to license wine casks. He alone could license the manufacture of the casks and no one could make such casks without a proper license. The monopoly holder got a fee for every license granted, of course, and often became fabulously wealthy.

A great uproar against the monopolies erupted in the early 1620's under King James. Public pressure at that time forced the King to cancel most of the monopolies. But under King Charles the monopolies came back in force. There were monopolies for:

-- the making of tobacco pipes.
-- the weighing of hay or straw.
-- the making of garments from beaver.
-- the measuring of corn, coal or salt.
-- the printing upon cloth.

4

Dozens of other monopolies were set up in a vast proliferation that inundated the country. The monopolists usually became rich. That was the idea. But the monopoly system placed a heavy burden on the public and a devastating brake on the economy.

For these, and other, reasons, Winthrop and his fellow Puritans felt that they must act. Conditions had become intolerable. There was no time to lose because all the signs indicated that God was about to inflict punishment on an erring nation. Winthrop saw himself as a man with a sacred duty. He had been called to lead a few of the chosen people to a place of refuge where they could escape God's wrath and provide a safe place for their Puritan church to put down roots. He must quit the corruption in England. He must emigrate with others into the wilderness of America where their True Faith could survive and flourish.[2]

Crossing the Ocean

All of these emigrants - whether rich or poor, pious or profane, honest or crooked - had to suffer the rigors of the ocean crossing. This was not an experience to be treated lightly. Only the crudest accommodations were available on the little sailing ships that traversed the Atlantic. Six to ten weeks cooped up on one of those vessels could be a nightmare.

[2] Many historians have assumed that the early colonists displayed exceptional courage in braving the perils of flight to America. The perils were great and the terrors were many. No question about that.

But James Truslow Adams takes a different view. He suggests that those who stayed behind in England displayed the greater bravery. The emigrant volunteer, Mr. Adams says, "showed a certain lack of courage when he decided that things had got too much for him at home." Because this is so, continues Mr. Adams, "it may be questioned whether those who remained in England, faced the conditions there including possible martydom, and fought the Stuart tyranny to a successful finish, were not the stronger."

This is one of those differences of opinion which we can debate but cannot settle. From this distance in time - more than three centuries - perhaps we can agree only that both those who emigrated and those who stayed home faced frightful risks. They lived in a period when danger was on every side. There simply weren't any easy paths to safety either for the emigrants or for those who stayed behind.

Generally the ships had a cavernous "room" in the hold just below the deck. The room was as long as the vessel. The floor was dirt spread over the rock ballast. The ceiling might be only five feet or so above the dirt floor. A fireplace occupied a position in the room with a hole in the deck above to let out some of the smoke.

This room provided passenger quarters for the emigrants. From fifty to one hundred and fifty men, women, and children would be crowded into the space. There was no privacy. In fact, the emigrants had to share the room with any goats, pigs, or cows making the trip. The animals were tethered at one end of the room but their presence was unmistakable.

Emmanuel Downing, who was familiar with these matters, advised a group of the 1630 emigrants that "by al means you should carrie a good store of garlicke to physicke your cows." This was considered an essential procedure to maintain the health of the cows. It was also a procedure that contributed to the mix of aromas in the hold and thus heightened passengers' discomfort.

The fleet that sailed with Governor Winthrop in 1630 started the voyage with two hundred cows. But they were "so tossed and brused" by the stormy trip that seventy of them perished before reaching America.

The shipboard diet of the emigrants was primitive and terribly monotonous. Mostly it was dried or salted meat, oatmeal porridge, and dried biscuits if the weevils hadn't ruined them. Water would go bad in the casks long before the voyage could be completed, so casks of beer were carried; this malted beverage did not go bad as quickly as did water.

Buckets were provided for calls of nature or for passengers retching with seasickness. From time to time, weather permitting, the buckets would be carried up to the deck and emptied overside. In rough weather when the hatches were closed, the passengers and the animals - including the "physicked" cows - were sealed off from fresh air and their compartment became a smoky, smelly cell.

On the larger ships, if notable passengers were making the crossing it was sometimes arranged to erect partitions in the hold to give the notables a little privacy. But on most of the crossings the passengers and the animals spent their days and their nights on that dirt floor in the one big communal dormitory.

Sickness was widespread - and it wasn't always just ordinary seasickness. The norm was several deaths per voyage. One ship, headed for Jamestown in 1618 started out with two hundred passengers; only fifty were alive when the ship reached America.

The little vessels were at the mercy of the wind, of course, and it was not unusual for them to be dead in the water for days when caught in a calm. Even when the wind was favorable, the clumsy craft moved only at a modest pace. Crossings that took eight to ten weeks were quite common. John Winthrop, Jr., son of the Massachusetts governor, made a crossing in 1642 aboard a merchantman named *An Cleeve*. From the time they left England the weather was unfavorable and it took them fourteen weeks to reach Boston.

The ship *Lyon* became celebrated for the number of successful crossings it made between England and Massachusetts. For many years it ran back and forth like a ferry boat. On one of these voyages the *Lyon* established a record when it carried seventy-three adults and fifty children to Boston without a fatality. It was the first recorded crossing of an emigrant vessel without a single loss of life.

Part of the *Lyon*'s success can be attributed to her master. He was one of the first sailing men to try out the notion that citrus fruit could prevent scurvy, the most common of shipboard ailments. This shipmaster carried a supply of lemon juice and he squirted it on all the food for his passengers and crew. The validity of the practice was proved a few centuries later when chemists, physicians, and nutritionists determined that vitamin C, abundant in citrus fruit, was indeed an effective agent to protect against scurvy.

Unbalanced populations

The colonists at Jamestown and at Plymouth stumbled into difficulties partly because of an unbalanced population mixture. While their numbers included many who could expound on the Bible, sit a horse, or handle a teacup with grace, there were precious few who knew how to catch a fish or dig a well. In short, there were too many gentlemen and too few workers. This is such a simple and obvious matter it seems strange that it could have been ignored so casually. But it was.

John Winthrop learned of this problem. Before he made his crossing in 1630 he interviewed Capt. John Smith and others who had experienced life in America. From them he learned the lesson that a successful colony must be balanced with workers and artisans skilled in all the chores the colonists would undertake. He kept this balance in mind as he recruited candidates for the Massachusetts Bay colony.

The essential diversity of skills in the community is illustrated by the allocation of house lots in Newbury in 1635. Lots were assigned to: three merchants, one sea captain, one dyer, one glover, four tanners, eight shoemakers, two wheelwrights, two blacksmiths, two linen weavers, two woolen weavers, one cooper, one saddler, one sawyer, three carpenters, one maltster, one physician, and one schoolmaster. The colony was completed with a handful of yeomen, thirty-odd unskilled workers – and eight gentlemen. (In Seventeenth Century society a gentleman was a person of means who performed no physical labor. He hired others to work for him while he dabbled in the arts, directed affairs from a desk, spent his time twiddling his thumbs, or simply loafed.)

The Howling Wilderness

The Puritans often they spoke of America as the howling wilderness. There were wolves in New England at the time and they may have done some howling from time to time, but the Puritans seem to have latched on to the "howling wilderness" term more as a catchy expression that somehow suited their fancy. They were familiar with the Biblical tales of brave souls going off into the wilderness to escape their enemies or to save their faith, and they gloried in the thought that by emigrating to America they would be emulating a notable Biblical example.

They also gloried in the comforting conceit that they were "God's chosen remnant", a people elected to carry on the True

Faith in a distant wilderness while God wreaked his punishment on a sinful England. America was sort of a redeployment base where the seeds of the True Faith could be planted, protected and made to flourish.

We can only guess how many of those early colonists shared the pious Governor Winthrop's religious zeal. Many of them did, certainly. Perhaps most did. It is accurate to point out, however, that some of these emigrants were moved less by religious piety than by other factors. Simple greed, for instance.

We must recognize, too, that something of a con game was going on here. Few of the emigrants knew what they were getting into for they had been conned into swallowing overblown tales. The early explorers, the ship captains, and the commercial men with financial interests in the growing colonies often exaggeratedly described the delights awaiting new-comers in America. A distorted picture was presented in England. The average Englishman heard only the glowing accounts of how salubrious the American climate was, how fertile the soil, how plentiful the fish and wild fowl - and don't forget those tempting rumors about the lavish abundance of gold, silver, and gems!

Thus, included among the early emigrants were some gullible souls who had been hoodwinked, and some others of an adventurous turn who were caught up in the glamor of moving to a new land where the attraction was not so much religious as it was romantic and economic.

Death Or Deportation

Still others emigrated for entirely different reasons.

The English courts often found it convenient to ship convicts to the colonies to get rid of them. There were occasions, too, when a judge would give a convicted criminal a choice of being hanged or being deported to America. So our community of early colonists in America included quite a few who had penal experience or who had emigrated to escape the gallows.

Indentured Servants

A considerable proportion of the first emigrants came over as indentured servants. These were people who wanted to emigrate to America but lacked the money for the fare. If they were reasonably strong and healthy they usually could find a sponsor and sign on as an indentured servant. The sponsor paid the fare. In return, the emigrant agreed to work without pay for the sponsor for a specified period, usually three to seven years. The sponsor was to provide food, clothing, and shelter, but no wage, during the period of indenture. Ship captains often bought the indenture papers, stood for the price of the fare, then sold the papers at a profit to a sponsor on the American side.

In many cases the indenture system worked satisfactorily. The indentured servant with a compassionate sponsor might be treated well and, at the end of his service, the servant might get a suit of clothes, a horse, a few acres of land, and some household tools from his sponsor. He was now on his own as a free man. In less happy circumstances, though, the indentured servants might be treated as slaves, beaten and

10

half-starved.

The indenture system also opened up opportunities for crooks, grafters, and cheats. Professional recruiters soon appeared on the scene. They moved through the pubs and back streets of London's slum districts signing up wastrels with glib promises. Once the victim was signed up as an indentured servant, the con man would deliver the victim to the dock and sell the indenture paper to a conniving ship captain.

Nor did the racket stop there. Recruiters bought children from worthless fathers or orphans from guardians and sold these children into bondage as indentured servants. On occasion, too, children were kidnapped off the street and delivered with forged papers to willing ship masters.

All this made for a broad variety among the emigrants who journeyed to America. It was a good deal broader and a sight more various than most of us are aware.

Abbott Emerson Smith, a well-informed student of the times, has put it this way:

The colonies were a haven for the Godly, a refuge for the oppressed, a challenge to the adventurous, but especially in regard to the indentured servants, the last resort of scoundrels, men and women who were dirty and lazy, rough, ignorant, lewd, and often criminal.

The First Troubles

In the beginning the Puritan colonists faced staggering trials. They had completed a long and difficult ocean crossing. Many of them were ill. Some of their number already had died at sea. Others, weakened by sickness and the paucity of food, would soon die and be buried in the New World. The little groups that straggled ashore in America were desperately in need of food and shelter. But where could they turn? There was no food market nearby, no lumber yard handy with a supply of boards and nails. For many weeks and months the colonists were compelled to suffer through severe food shortages and to depend for shelter on riverbank caves or rude huts fashioned with saplings and sod.

There was wild game in the forest and fish in the sea, but it took time for the colonists to learn how to hunt and fish in this strange land. They had brought with them seeds to plant, but must count months before the land could be cleared, the seeds planted, and crops harvested. They also had brought over with them some sheep, goats, and cows, though many of these domestic animals did not survive the ocean crossing and many of those that did had difficulty adjusting to the new habitat.

That first period of settlement thus was a time in which illness was rife, starvation was close at hand, and the level of suffering was intense.

One of the many little ships which made the crossing to Massachusetts Bay in 1630 was the *Mary and John*. She landed her one hundred and forty passengers, and livestock just below Boston at a place they named Dorchester. The hardships this little group suffered in that first year are typical. They are described in an account left by Roger Clap, a passenger on the *Mary and John* and historian for the settlement. Here is his report of that first year at Dorchester:

Oh the hunger that man suffered, and saw no hope in the eye of reason to be supplied, only by clams, muscles (sic) and fish. We did quietly build boats, and some went a-fishing but bread with many was a scarce thing, and flesh of all kinds scarce. And in these days in our straits, though I cannot say 'God sent a raven to feed us, as he did the prophet Elijah' yet this I can say to the praise of God's glory, that He sent not only poor, ravenous Indians, which came with their baskets of corn on their backs to trade with us, which was a good supply unto many; but also sent ships from Holland and Ireland, and provisions and Indian corn from Virginia, to supply the wants of his dear servants in the Wilderness, both with food and raiment. And when people's wants were great, not only in our town but in diverse towns, such was the goodly wisdom, care and prudence of our Governor Winthrop and his assistants, that when a ship came loaded with provisions, they did order that the whole cargo should be bought for a general stock, and so accordingly it was, and distribution was made to every town and every person in each town, as every man had need. Thus God was pleased to comfort His people in time of straits, and to fill His servants with food and gladness. Then did all the servants of God bless His holy name and loved one another, fervently.

Three significant points come clear in this account by Mr. Clap. First, there were friendly Indians in the neighborhood who came "with their baskets of corn on their backs to trade with us" at a time when the colonists were desperately in need of grain. If the Indians had not been friendly – if instead of bringing in corn for the half-starved colony they had at-

12

tacked the colonists – the history of the New World may have been entirely different.

The second significant point in Mr. Clap's account is the success of Governor Winthrop in devising a communal system to allocate food for the entire colony. In a later age, this arrangement might be viewed as a form of communism. But whatever the system might be called, it worked. Whenever a ship came in with a load of provisions, the governor had it taken over so that the entire supply could be allocated fairly to all the residents in all the various Bay settlements. If the governor had not acted in this fashion, the likelihood is – human nature being what it is – that a few smart operators would have gained control of the shipment, created a monopoly, and made themselves rich at the expense of the colony's poorest families.

The third point is the thread of piety that runs through Mr. Clap's report. Like all the Puritan leaders, Mr. Clap was deeply religious. It was customary in the Puritan society to couch even the most routine accounts in pious terms with Biblical references and frequent thanks to God for the comforts He had brought to His servants. Thus Mr. Clap's account of the colony's troubles with its many references to God conforms to the accepted pattern.

The death tolls were appalling in the infant settlement. Of the one hundred and two passengers who crossed on the *Mayflower* in 1620 and landed at Plymouth, fifty-two died during the first winter. At Massachusetts Bay, two hundred of the colonists who made the crossing in the migration of 1630 died before the spring of 1631.

One of the original settlers at Hartford lamented his sorry condition in 1634. He echoed the plight of the many who shared his suffering and his despondency.

"The tymes are dangerous, our beginnings raw, our encumbrances great, necessities many, our helps few and these weak."

Sights and Smells

We Twentieth Century people would be shocked, confused, and appalled if a time machine somehow should manage to transport us back to Seventeenth Century New England. Oh, there would be some things we could admire. The woods, streams, and beaches were relatively pristine and no man-made smog contaminated the air. But if we should venture

13

into the communities, the scene would be less agreeable. Here we surely would be dismayed by the sights and repelled by the smells.

The Puritans were rugged folks living out rugged lives. Their looks and their manners were alien to anything we are familiar with today. We would find them crude, dirty, smelly, egotistical, and nauseatingly righteous. Even their speech was a Seventeenth Century dialect which we would find almost as unintellible as a foreign tongue. If we try to draw a truthful picture there is no way to avoid this unhappy judgment.

Charles Francis Adams, Jr. was one of the first historians to examine the colonial period without the customary romantic illusions. Writing in 1890, Mr. Adams reported:

"The earliest times in New England were not pleasant, and the earlier generations were not pleasant to live with. One accustomed to the variety, luxury and refinement of modern life (as of 1890) would, if carried back suddenly into the admired existence of the past, experience an acute and lasting attack of homesickness and disgust."

That probably is an accurate assessment. Early colonial homes often were shacks with dirt floors. Even the finest dwellings were heated only with fireplaces. Food was cooked at the fireplace and usually eaten with the fingers.

Clothing was apt to be badly soiled because it was so seldom washed. The people also seldom washed. A belief prevailed at the time that water was harmful and weakening whether taken internally or applied externally. As a result, beer, rum, and hard cider were the preferred drinks and few people took baths.

The widespread aversion to water was not just a silly habit. Typhoid fever and a variety of intestinal ills were caused by contaminated water, and one could never be sure about the purity of water from spring or well in the villages. Even small children drank watered-down potions of beer or cider. Yet in spite of these precautions, intestinal illness was as common as the common cold and the death toll from illness was appalling.

The Class System

Another reason – a subtle one – for shunning drinking water was a product of the English class system. Anyone in England at the time who could afford to spend a few pence drank rum, wine, beer, or cider. Only the poor and the destitute drank water as the common animals did. People of means thus flaunted their position in the class system by spurning the pauper's drinking water.

The class system was one of the English practices brought over intact by the early colonists. Later on it would be worn down, trimmed, amended, and pretty well eliminated, but in the early years the colonists in America lived under a sharply stratified social system exactly like the system in England. The fundamental thought was that there was a class born to rule, and another class born "to be ruled and not to rule others." Each person's class was established at birth and that was that. All manual labor was to be performed by the lower classes. A gentleman never soiled his hands with toil; he was upper class.

Church pews were alloted strictly according to the wealth, influence and class of the parishioners. Even clothing reflected class. Members of the lower classes were forbidden to wear clothing deemed suitable only for citizens of higher rank. The sumptuary laws forbade the lower orders "to take upon them the garb of gentlemen, or to walk in great boots, or women of the same rank to wear taffeta hoods, although allowed to persons of greater estate or more liberal education."

The wife of John Hutchins of Newbury, Massachusetts, was arrested in 1633 on the charge that she was caught in public wearing a silken hood. The charge was dismissed, however, when the court heard testimony that Mrs. Hutchins, before her marriage, "had been brought up above the ordinary rank." In other words, her rank, established at birth, entitled her to wear clothing denied to ordinary commoners.

Remnants of this caste system hung on in America for more than a century. As late as 1759, Boston considered a particular candidate for justice of the peace was not qualified because his grandfather had been a bricklayer.

The practice of bathing was as slow to catch on as was a more tolerant attitude toward social class. About seventy-five years after the Puritans first settled around Boston, some of the wealthier families began installing bath houses on their property. The bath house was a mark of status. But bathing was still an uncommon diversion far into the 1700's both in England and in America. Samuel Pepys, writing in London in the mid-1600's, expressed astonishment when his wife informed him that not only had she taken a bath but planned to take another one soon.

Elizabeth Drinker, the wife of an eminent Quaker in Philadelphia, Pennsylvania, had a shower bath installed in her

15

backyard in 1799 for therapeutic reasons. She tried it out and confided in her diary:

"I bore it better than expected, not having been wett all over at once for 28 years past."

Privy and Chamber Pot

This was the period of the privy and the chamber pot. It was also a period with an informal lack of arrangement for disposing of waste. One walked carefully on the streets to avoid garbage and excrement.

The town meeting at Newport, Rhode Island, addressed a bothersome situation in 1707. It appears in the record as follows:

"Several Privy Houses sett against ye cosways or pavements when people pass...spoiling peoples apparill should they happen to be near when ye filfth comes out...especially in ye night when people cannot see to shun them."[3]

Who Needs Roads?

Our early colonists couldn't care less about roadways. They had more serious matters than road building to contend with in the New World, matters such as food and shelter and survival. In fact, most of the emigrants had never seen a good road or considered such a road's worth. When Romans invaded England, they built many miles of durable, well-engineered roads but these were later neglected and fell into disrepair. By the Seventeenth Century, the roads in England were a network of pot-holed, rock-strewn thoroughfares often ankle-deep in mud in bad weather. This situation was generally accepted, though; no one showed the slightest inter-

[3] Colonial manuscripts often have the word "ye" where we would use the word "the." The colonial practice stems from an Anglo-Saxon letter which was called "thorn" and was pronounced "th. The original letter called thorn looked something like our small letter "b" with a tail added at the bottom. That original letter became extinct. Then colonial writers began substituting the letter "y" for the extinct thorn as sort of a shorthand meaning "th ." The colonial "ye" was pronounced "the," not "yee."

est in improving them. There was no widespread complaint, no demands for corrective action.

Queen Elizabeth had a fancy horse-drawn carriage, the first one ever built in England. It was one of her prized possessions and she enjoyed showing it off before the admiring populace. Drawn by two horses, it made a splendid display. Except at the royal stables, however, horse-drawn wheeled vehicles were rare in early Seventeenth Century England. Travelers either walked or rode horses because wheeled vehicles would have found the going too difficult on those muddy, pot-holed roads. (The Queen never traveled far in her fancy carriage. It was just for show, not utility.)

So it was that when the colonists reached New England they had never seen any good roads, were not aware of any value in a road system, and had plenty of more critical problems to contend with before they would even consider the lesser matter of roads through the forests. All of the first colonists settled on waterways. These waterways were their "roads" and most of their transportation was by boat.

There were some pathways in the forests and the colonists sometimes used them. Usually these paths were called Indian trails and probably the Indians used them when it suited them to do so. But it is unlikely that many of them were actually laid out by Indians. More likely, they were traced originally by deer or other wild animals seeking water or forage, or perhaps they were just haphazard clearings in the forest formed by nature.

We do know, though, that some of the colonists did some impressive walking, whether along Indian trails or not. For example, the several score colonists from Dorchester and Boston who set out in 1635 to find new homes in the Connecticut Valley made the trip west on foot. The straight line distance of their trek is only about ninety miles, but since they had to get over streams, around ponds, over hills and through dense woods, they must have done a lot of zig-zagging and the total distance of their trip may have been one hundred and thirty miles or more. They were handicapped too, because they took along with them their herd of cattle. The journey took two weeks.

Roger Clap has described that migration to the Connecticut in vivid terms:

Never before had the forests of America witnessed such a scene as this, driving their cattle before them – the compass their only guide – through the bewildering mazes of the unbroken forest, commencing and ending each day's

17

march with songs of praise and heartfelt utterances of prayer.

It was a difficult and memorable trip, but they made it. And at their destination on the Connecticut River, the migrants separated into three groups and established three communities: Hartford, Wethersfield, and Windsor.

The colonists sometimes walked from one settlement to another following the so-called Indian trails. On such walks it was advisable to carry along a stout axe to clear away brush or limbs that blocked the trail.

Governor Winthrop, in his journal, casually records a time when he walked the thirty-five miles or so down the coast to pay a call on his friends in Plymouth. He regarded the thirty-five-mile hike as just a pleasant stroll.

For the vast majority of the colonists, however, there was no time for pleasant strolls to the next settlement. They were farmers and artisans whose work kept them fully occupied from sunup to sundown. A fifty-mile journey was a once-in-a-lifetime experience for a few, and many colonists lived out their whole lives without ever venturing more than a dozen miles from their place of birth.

Later on, many of the Indian trails were sufficiently beaten down and broadened so that they could be used by riders on horseback and by pack trains. Many decades were to pass, however, before the roads in America could accommodate wagons, carriages and stagecoaches. By the time of the American Revolution in 1776, a crude network of dirt roads linked most of the settlements along the north Atlantic coast. But the first stagecoach didn't appear until 1785. It ran between New York City and Albany.

A Period of Plenty

Gradually the hardships of building a colony from scratch were overcome. Trees were felled and gardens planted, sturdy dwellings were erected, boats were built, fishing was pursued, and wild game was shot or trapped for furs or food.

Indian corn proved an unexpected blessing. It didn't require a broad, tilled field. Set out in hills, the corn could be planted among the stumps of felled trees and it provided an abundant crop for man and beast. Even the corn stalks, after the ears had been removed, made good fodder for the cattle. The colonists also adopted the sensible and efficient Indian practice of planting beans and pumpkins amid the corn hills; the bean runners climbed the corn stalks.

After a few years of strenuous toil, the Puritan colony was able to count its blessings. Starvation no longer was an immediate problem because food supplies were ample. Housing was vastly improved. The community had reached a level of stability and relative prosperity. Moreover, the outlook was bright for even greater improvements.

At this time a happenstance occured which illustrated the colony's relative well-being.

For many years British seamen had made a regular practice of stopping for fresh supplies at colonies in the West Indies. Fruits and vegetables were abundant in these islands – not to mention the fresh water, sugar, and rum. But in 1647 a serious drought killed off crops in the West Indies. It spread despair through the islands. When visiting British seamen, low on supplies, learned that they could not replenish their stocks in the Indies they set a course for New England not knowing what to expect. To their surprise and delight they found the New Englanders had amassed impressive surpluses of grain, fish, cheese, and other goods. This turn of affairs moved Governor Winthrop to gloat:

"Many of the London seamen were wont to despise New England as a poor, barren country but now they are relieved by our plenty."

It was about this time, too, that the Massachusetts General Court – probably prodded by the Governor – found it expedient to assure a skeptical government in London that "God hath blessed this countrey with food of all kinds." The statement was inscribed in a formal resolution and forwarded to England in an attempt to confound any remaining doubters there.

Strong roots had been planted. They were nourished by the

toil of hard–working colonists. The colony prospered. Saw mills, grist mills, and shipyards were established. Boats were built and sent to the fishing grounds off the Grand Banks. Dried fish and grain were shipped to the West Indies in exchange for sugar and rum. Timber, fish, and naval stores, such as hemp and pine pitch for ship-caulking, were sent to England in exchange for manufactured items. By the 1650's, Edward Johnson was moved to praise the dramatic transformation wrought by the Puritan colonists:

"The remote, rocky, barren, bushy wild–woody wilderness has become a second England for fertilness in so short a space that it is indeed the wonder of the world. The close, clouded woods have become goodly corn fields. Wolves and bears nurst up their young in those very places where today the streets now are full of Girles and Boys sporting up and down with continual concourse of people."

The Sea Beckons

It was inevitable that the colonists at Massachusetts Bay would gravitate toward the sea. Some time would pass before the lesson was fully appreciated, but gradually they learned that the rough, rocky soil of New England was suitable only for small crops - there could be no cash crop like the tobacco of Virginia or the sugar in the Indies - and that while fur-trapping and -trading were useful sidelines, they never could be as successful in the Massachusetts area as they were farther inland and farther north. Coastal New England's future prosperity must depend on the sea.

At the start, the colonists probed waters of the bay for crabs, clams, lobsters, and shallow-water fish. Dorchester, tapping the skills of some of their number who had fished off the southern coast of England, managed to build a few small boats in which men fished farther out in the bay. Indeed, Dorchester claims to have had the first fishing fleet in Massachusetts Bay - and perhaps the claim is justified if we can count as a "fleet" a batch of dory-like small boats, mostly oared but a few adorned with mast and sail.

From this simple beginning, however, the fishing, boat-building, and shipping industries grew step by step until they had become the dominant industries in New England.

Several preliminary steps were necessary. Sawmills had to be set up to provide planking. Weavers had to be established

20

to provide sailcloth. Lumbermen had to be employed to turn out masts and spars. All this was accomplished in time.

The codfish which swam in great schools offshore became a major item in the colonial economy. Salted and dried, the cod was useful at home and extremely valuable as a commodity in trade. Fishermen from Europe had been catching cod off the northern coasts of America for decades. It was perfectly understandable, therefore, that the colonists would direct much of their attention toward fishing for cod.

As the little shipyards began to appear in coastal communities, a major interest was in building vessels sturdy and able enough to sail to the offshore banks where the water teemed with cod.

In some of the ports – Marblehead, for example – fleets of vessels were built exclusively for the fishing trade. Small boys in those communities had only one goal: they lived for the day when they would be big enough to sign on as cabin boys or deckhands on those risky fishing trips off to the banks. That was the life of glamor and excitement.

But just when the prospects seemed to be improving, when the ship builders were getting more efficient and the fishing industry was flourishing, New England was plunged into an economic depression. The cause was the outbreak of civil war in England in 1641. A mutually beneficial trade came to an abrupt end because the civil war put a clamp on commerce and virtually halted all ship movements between England and her American colonies. No longer could colonists get the products they had been receiving regularly from England; no longer could they trade their surplus goods in England as had been their custom.

Governor Winthrop bemoaned the desperate situation. "All foreign commodities grew scarce," he wrote later, "and our own of no price (value). Corn would buy nothing. A cow which last year cost Ł20 might be bought for Ł4 or Ł5. These straits set our people on work to provide fish, clapboards, plank, etc., and to look to the West Indies for trade."

Look to the Indies

In this time of trouble, the colonists discovered that their commercial hopes now lay in their governor's advice to "look to the West Indies for a trade."

Bustling settlements had developed on the Caribbean Islands in the West Indies. The earliest European colonists came from Spain, France, England, Portugal, Holland, and Denmark. But whatever their country of origin, once the Europeans had a toehold in the New World, they showed similar patterns of settlement: first they annihilated or enslaved the local Indians, then they established feudal economies; when they ran short of local slaves, they sought others elsewhere, importing thousands of blacks from Africa.

As time ran on, the Islanders learned that their greatest benefit accrued from specializing in a single product. It had to be a product suited to the climate, capable of being planted, tended and harvested by slave labor, and a product in broad demand in distant markets. Sugar cane was ideal.

The emphasis on a one-crop economy had its advantages. But the other side of this coin was equally apparent: the greater the degree of one-crop specialization, the greater became the Islanders' dependency on outside sources for most of their basic necessities.

This was a situation made to order for the New Englanders and they were alert enough to take quick advantage of it. Thus it was that when the civil war cut off commerce with England, the New Englanders turned to the Caribbean. Trade between Massachusetts and the West Indies grew rapidly. Puritan New England became the principal supplier of cattle, lumber, salted fish, and other provisions for the Indies. The Islanders in the Indies became more and more dependent on New England for their necessary imports.

Still another benefit went to New England. As the trade flourished, the shipping merchants in Boston achieved dominant control over the distribution of all the products from the West Indies. In addition to the quantities of sugar, there were appreciable amounts of coffee, oranges, ginger, and pepper. Some of the Indies sugar acquired in trade was shipped directly to foreign ports. Some went to New England to be converted into rum. (At a somewhat later date, New England counted sixty-seven distilleries, every one of them busily producing rum for domestic use or for foreign trade.)

The significant point is that this whole business – the buying, trading, conversion, shipping, and selling – rested in the hands of merchants with headquarters in Boston. The profits were enormous.

Shipbuilding activity in Massachusetts expanded rapidly. By 1660, shipbuilding had become a leading industry. There were shipyards at Newbury, Ipswich, Gloucester, Salem, and Boston. Vessels were now being turned out in great variety and in large numbers: there were little shallops capable of carrying a couple of men and a few bags of grain from one settlement to another, forty- or fifty-footers for the coastal trade, and larger vessels for fishing expeditions out to the banks and for trading at distant ports in the West Indies or in Europe.

The forests at hand provided an ample supply of oak and pine. Rope walks were established. Hempen sailcloth was produced on hand looms. Anchors were forged and fashioned from bog iron.

So successful were the Yankee shipbuilders that their activity began to pinch shipbuilders in England. This didn't sit well. English commercial men thought it was proper for the colonies to provide raw materials such as masts, spars, hemp, and pitch, but they were sharply annoyed by the prospect of the colonies providing whole ships. That was considered unfair competition.

We have here the genesis of a matter that would plague the colonial powers repeatedly in the years to follow. The original thought of the empire builders was that the colonies were fated to provide only raw materials. That was what colonies were for. That was the natural order. It was the mother country's exclusive privilege and duty to take those raw materials and convert them into manufactured goods for export.

The trouble was that things got sticky when the colonists departed from the natural order and began manufacturing things from their own raw materials. In the eyes of the merchantmen in England, that is precisely what these upstart New Englanders were now beginning to do in the shipbuilding industry. Complaints were loud and demands for corrective relief were numerous.

But no matter how much the commercial men in England might protest, there was no stopping the colonists. The New England Yankees had found their niche. They were well on their way to becoming shipbuilders and seafarers who would make their mark around the globe.

Yankee Smugglers

The New England Puritans, as subjects of the King of England, were quite meticulous in observing most of the royal laws most of the time. Generally they rendered unto Caesar what Caesar demanded.

But there was an important exception. When the Puritans got a deck under them and sailed off to sea their attitude changed. No longer did they bow in humble acceptance. No longer did they feel the constraints of London's laws. Evasion of the royal shipping laws was widely regarded by the Puritan Yankees as an enjoyable and profitable practice. No matter how much it might be denounced in royal quarters, it found broad acceptance in the new Yankee lexicon.

The government in England had set up a lengthy list of laws designed to keep the colonies under firm control. The idea was to make sure that the profits from the colonial trade passed directly to proper pockets in London. There was a law, for example which required that every single pound of American-grown tobacco be shipped directly to England where English merchants could handle it. Another law made it illegal for the colonists to trade directly with Spain - or with any other nation with which England happened to be spatting.

It didn't take the colonists long, though, to figure out ways to sneak around these burdensome laws. Some of the ways showed great ingenuity. One successful ploy dreamed up at Massachusetts Bay started out by sending a fleet of little coasting shallops down into Chesapeake Bay. Quantities of tobacco were purchased at Chesapeake ports and loaded on the shallops. The tobacco then was carried to Boston, transferred to larger vessels and sent over to Spain. There it was traded for wine and other items and the whole lot was taken back to

Boston. According to the English royal laws, this whole business was strictly illegal, of course, but it provided employment for many colonists and attractive profits for Yankee seamen and Boston merchants, so the bold New England traders continued to thumb their noses at these particular royal bans.

Smuggling in various forms persisted as an honorable calling for many colonial merchants and ship owners. The Yankees were beginning to feel their oats. They were learning to cherish their independence and to appreciate the profits of their own initiative, and they refused to let any silly directive from a distant government in London interfere with their lucrative operations. Some colonial fortunes were founded on the smuggling trade.

Yet despite the widespread smuggling, which caused vast annoyance in London, the English government did achieve some success in its main goal. After it had settled its civil war and settled down, it managed to control much of the trade with America.

Louis M. Hacker says the two-way trade developed slowly as the colonies were struggling to their feet but soon reached impressive proportions. By the time of the Revolution, Mr. Hacker estimates that the American colonies were consuming one-third of all England's exports. England was sending out to the colonies quantities of iron ware, textiles, house furnishings, paper, and books. In return, England was taking in timber, masts, naval stores (such as turpentine, pitch, and hemp), fish, furs, potash, and tobacco.

It was mostly a comfortable arrangement. But, again, the situation based, originally, on collaboration became a situation seething with competition. England found its colonies getting out of hand. The New Englanders particularly were acting up. They were making their own rules and paying less and less attention to directives from London. Relations became increasingly abrasive, and the showdown would come with the Revolutionary War.

Winthrop Challenged

Throughout most of this period – from the earliest days of hardship up to the days of relative prosperity – Governor Winthrop presided as the colony's chief magistrate. He was held in great respect. His leadership and his force of character surely were imporant factors contributing to the colony's success.

Nevertheless, the governor's twelve terms in office were not consecutive, nor were they blessed by a perpetual aura of sweetness and light. There were occasions when Governor Winthrop's judgment was questioned. Indeed, there were two occasions when dissidents got the upper hand and the governor was evicted from office.

At the start, Winthrop was elected governor and Thomas Dudley was elected deputy governor. Winthrop was forty-two years old in 1630; Dudley was fifty-four. The two could not be considered a harmonious pair. They were at odds as often as they were in agreement. Both were proud, able, and forceful, and steeped in arrogance. The spats between them spread out over a period of years and frequently became sufficiently furious to give off sparks.

At the time the ruling body in Massachusetts was called the General Court. It consisted of a governor, a deputy governor, twelve assistants to the governor, and the freemen. The freemen were like stockholders in a corporation or like voters at a town meeting. Any man who owned property which could be taxed and who was a member of the church would be accepted as a freeman. Elections were held annually. The entire body, including all the freemen, would elect the governor, the deputy governor, and the twelve assistants to serve the new one-year term.

An especially bitter debate over the Court broke out in 1634. Rumors spread among the freemen that Governor Winthrop had exceeded his authority. Some though he was acting like a dictator. Two principal demands were made by the protesting freemen. First, they wanted to see the colony's official charter (which was held in a safe and never put on public display) to find out just how much power had been assigned to the governor. Second, they demanded that all basic legislation be vested in the General Court as a whole, not merely in the hands of the governor and his assistants. (Thomas Dudley may not have instigated this uproar personally, but he became a participant and ultimately a beneficiary.)

The freemen won both of their demands. First, they were permitted to examine the colony's charter - and they decided that the Governor had not exceeded his authority. Second, the decision was agreed that henceforth all basic legislative action would be handled by the entire General Court, not merely the court's leaders. Then the rebellious freemen topped off their victory by ousting Winthrop from the governor's chair and installing Dudley.

A minor result of the squabble was that the capital of the

colony was shifted from Boston (Winthrop's home village) over to Newtown (where Dudley resided). Dudley had argued for years that Newtown was the proper place for the capital. He finally achieved this transfer when he won his place in the governor's chair. (The name Newtown later was changed to Cambridge.) Dudley served only one term as Governor, however. After that term, Winthrop was put back in the Governor's chair, the court returned to Boston where it remains today, and Dudley was demoted to deputy.

Another political dispute broke out in 1636. This time Winthrop was ousted again and Sir Henry Vane was elected governor. Vane's term was brief, however. He lasted in office only a year, then quit the colony in disgust and sailed back to England.

These two instances turned out to be only brief pauses in Governor Winthrop's career as a leader. In each case he was re-elected to office after a short time as a political "out."

Mrs. Sherman's Sow

Mrs. O'Leary's cow earned a footnote in history when it kicked over the lantern and started the Great Chicago Fire of 1871.

Mrs. Sherman's sow almost achieved similar notoriety in Boston. It didn't start any fire, but it did figure in a rancorous quarrel before the General Court of Massachusetts in 1643 which set something of a precedent.

Pigs and other domestic animals often roamed the lanes of Boston in this period. The animals frequently got loose and took off on foraging expeditions if the owners did not keep their fences in repair.

Mrs. Sherman was a widow of ordinary estate. She could not bother to fuss with fences, and as a result her outsized sow spent more time prowling the neighborhood than it did in its pen. Folks in the area generally didn't object. The sow caused them no bother.

But there came a day when a gentleman dandy, Captain Keayne, had an encounter with Mrs. Sherman's sow. The captain was striding along the lane, headed for the village center, when his course by chance took him close by Mrs. Sherman's sow. Now the sow had been wallowing blissfully in a deep mud hole that morning. Just as the captain approached, the sow chose that moment to stand up and shake off some of the sloppy accumulations on her hide. Some splotches of mud landed on the captain's otherwise immaculate trousers. One large glob even landed squarely on his new waistcoat.

The captain was livid. He filed a formal complain against Mrs. Sherman and when he got no satisfaction he carried his complaint right up to the General Court.

When the matter of Captain Keayne and the sow came up, the governor, the deputy governor, and the assistants all sided with the captain. They knew him as a high-born citizen of some consequence. But the forty or so freemen were virtually unanimous in siding with Mrs. Sherman. She was their kind of person, not a hoity-toity snob. The class conflict here was obvious. The captain represented the upper class whereas Mrs. Sherman made no pretense of being other than an ordinary widow of the lower class.

After several hours of noisy argument, Governor Winthrop and his aides decided on a radical step to quiet the storm: they would divide the General Court. The governor, his deputy, and the assistants met in one room; the freemen from the villages held their own meeting in another room. Such a separation, the leaders felt, would at least lower the level of insult and imprecation and perhaps help toward working out a solution.

Just what happened to Captain Keayne, Mrs. Sherman, and the sow does not come clear. There are political scientists, however, who see in that decision to divide the General Court the first step toward creating the bicameral legislative system which was to become a fixture in government. Here was a milestone in civics and a pig was responsible. Simple justice suggests that Mrs. Sherman's sow deserves a place in history up there somewhere near Mrs. O'Leary's cow.

Schools Established

The settlers at Massachusetts Bay put a high value on education. A large proportion of them were literate, many with university training, and they were determined to continue the colony's literate standing.

J. C. Furnas surmises that the Bay colony had much the most cultivated population of all the early settlements in America. "Except for hired and indentured servants," he writes, "probably all the Puritans arriving in 1630 could read and write, and the ratio of university graduates to total population was higher than in any nation then or today." That's an interesting observation, but one difficult to prove. Available evidence does indicate, however, the serious place that schooling occupied in the Puritan communities. It was a genuine commitment, not just a passing fad.

In 1647 a law was enacted requiring that every town in the Bay colony with fifty households must employ a teacher to teach the three R's, and every community with one hundred families must also establish a grammar school. That was the start of the public school system in America.

At the lowest level, the town teacher taught youngsters to read. At the next level, the grammar school accepted an elite group of boys - selected as much for social standing as for scholarly prowess - and taught them the languages needed to study theology and the humanities. Finally, the more promising young students from the grammar school went on to Harvard to receive training for the ministry or for politics.

The establishment of Harvard College in 1636 demonstrated the deeply-felt interest the Puritans had in education. At a time when the Puritan settlements were struggling with the basic problems of food, shelter, and safety - indeed, were struggling for survival - these determined colonists found the courage to start building a college.

Surely there were critics in the colony who looked upon this college idea as utter foolishness. Surely there were dissenters who could argue that food for the body at this critical juncture was far more essential than food for the soul. But the critics and the dissenters were put down. A grant was authorized by the General Court to initiate the project, a site was chosen on the Charles River at New Towne (later renamed Cambridge), and work began on the college. The first buildings went up in 1637 and the first class graduated in 1642.

Meanwhile, in 1639, the college's endowment was increased with a substantial gift from John Harvard. In gratitude, the colony named the institution Harvard College.

Yale, which would become a long-time rival of Harvard, came into being at least partly because of a case of sour grapes. Cotton Mather was a distinguished clergyman in the late 1600's. He had graduated from Harvard in 1681, and one of his fondest desires was to follow his father, Increase Mather, in the Harvard College presidency. But this was not to be. He was passed over by the Harvard board. So Cotton Mather, stung by failure, began agitating for another college. He and a group of other clergymen finally brought this off in 1701 when they founded the Collegiate School of America at Saybrook, Connecticut. It was moved later to New Haven, and after getting a large bequest from Elihu Yale was renamed for that generous benefactor. Cotton Mather served as a trustee at Yale, but never as its president.

* * * * *

Some colonies in the New World less-favored than Massachusetts Bay had high proportions of slaves, indentured servants, and convicts among their first settlers. Indeed, Charles A. and Mary R. Beard write: "It seems probable that at least one-half of the immigrants into America before the Revolution, certainly outside New England, were either indentured servants or Negro slaves."

If those levels were so high, it follows that the levels of literacy in those colonies probably were correspondingly low. For years to come, the problem of schooling and the general level of education would be matters of concern in those settlements. Ultimately school systems were established in all of the colonies, and it was the Puritans in New England who planted the first seeds.

Among the colonists were a few with a special bent for scholarly research. Numbered in this group was John Winthrop, Jr., son of the Massachusetts governor. The younger Winthrop was a political leader. He served on the General Court at Boston. Later, in 1657, he became the first governor of Connecticut. While governor, he was a mediator who helped bring about the peaceful transition from New Amsterdam to New York.

Yet though his political activities were many and varied, he did not pursue them exclusively. He was a great reader, and his collection of some one thousand volumes was considered the largest private library in America. He was also a naturalist of some competence. He found time to study the flora, fauna, and geography of New England, and he was appointed a correspondent in America for the British Royal Society.

Winthrop collected quantities of specimens for study and shipped them off to fellow scholars in England. (The shells of horseshoe crabs he had found on the Massachusetts beaches caused consternation in the mother country for no

30

such creature had ever been seen there.) Winthrop also had a small telescope. He scanned the heavens with this instrument and wrote several treatises about his astronomical findings.

It's a pity that the younger John Winthrop and Ben Franklin happened along in different centuries. Both had a deep fascination with science and natural history and they would have made congenial neighbors.

CHAPTER TWO

PURITAN RELIGION

Our Puritan ancestors were human beings, of course, and as such they had all the customary human emotions. It follows that they must have known moments of joy as well as moments of sadness. But where was the joyousness? If it was there, it was carefully hidden because the record that comes down to us depicts a people toiling grimly from day to day in a society that as studiously shunned enjoyment as it shunned the plague. The accepted Puritan belief was that if an activity gave pleasure it was necessarily sinful. And these were pious people.

The true church, the Puritans believed, must be a stern church. It must hew to the Biblical word and follow standards of worship established at the time of Jesus. The ministers must be saintly figures without flaw. Parishioners must be forced to accept and conform.

Plainness was associated with piety. There could be no elaborate ceremony, no painted windows on churches, no statues of saints, no incense, no ritual candles.

Puritan weddings were conducted without music and without wedding rings – because music was regarded as a profane intrusion and rings were shunned as pagan gadgetry. Puritan funerals were short, simple, grim. Christmas was just another day of toil. Christ's birthday was recognized, but the Puritans banned any form of celebration on that day because they considered the merriment associated with Yule festivities back in England to be heathen practices concocted in the devil's workshop.

Many generations were to pass before the strict Puritan society loosened its bans and permitted the Christmas tree, the exchange of gifts, and the joyous Yuletide music to become acceptable forms of celebration. Indeed, not until the 1800's did the celebration of Christmas in New England begin to take on the forms we are accustomed to today.

Partying – a Sin

In none of the Puritan communities did the folks gather simply to have fun. Fun was a no-no. Partying was frowned upon as sinful. Dancing and card-playing were strictly prohibited. So were stage plays. These strait-laced descendants of William Shakespeare disdainfully regarded the stage as a play pen for the devil's disciples.

The ban on stage plays hung on for more than a century. In 1748 British officers posted in Boston got together and staged an occasional play to eke out their low wages. They got away with it for a while. Then the Puritan authorities awoke to the perils of this pandering with Satan and stepped in. The plays were banned.

Once in a while the Puritan families did assemble for occasions at which, one may suppose, there was some opportunity for laughing, joking or horseplay – perhaps even a little flirting. But these gatherings always had a serious purpose. There was the sugaring-off festival in the spring, for instance, and the corn-husking bee in the fall. Such gatherings had the blessing of the authorities – provided, of course, that they were conducted in a manner that did not offend the delicate sensibilities of the Puritan moralists.

The picture the leaders sought to present was a picture of a God-fearing community in which the highest moral tone prevailed and no devilish levity was tolerated.

What they wanted and what they got, however, were two quite different kettles of soup. The colonial records are so full of instances of drunkenness, immoral conduct, and unwanted pregnancies that one is forced to conclude quite a bit of unpublicized partying went on behind the pious facade of Puritanism. Some students of the matter have even become convinced that the repressive pressures imposed by the strict Puritan codes of conduct, far from raising the moral tone of the community, actually encouraged immorality. The record lends support to this point of view. One daring estimate even suggests that a third of the babies born in Puritan New England were illegitimate.

Robert C. Black III has written the following about conditions in the New Haven, Connecticut, colony:

> *There was a profound and unhealthy concern with sexual matters, in particular the lapses of others, and any misconduct was investigated, and officially set down, in such detail that a number of the 17th Century records of New Haven have yet to see 20th Century print.*

The high-spirited capers of Puritan young men led to the first speed law enacted in America. In the spring of 1669, Connecticut authorities found it necessary to crack down on the show-offs who, in their search for excitement, had taken to spurring their horses through the communities at breakneck speed.

The new speed law was directed at those "who are apt to be injurious to their neighbors by their disorderly riding in the townes, whereby the lives of themselves and others are hazarded and endangered." It restricted riders to "an ordinary and easy hand gallop." Violators faced a fine of five shillings.

This came at a time when population congestion and its attendan inconveniences were beginning to be felt in the little clusters of buildings that formed the "townes." Windsor's population had swelled to seven hundred and fifty-four. Hartford's was seven hundred and twenty-one. They were the two most populous communities in Connecticut, much too populous to permit dare-devil racing through the village center.

That problem of youthful speeders would recur in later years with the scorchers on bicycles, the leather-jacketed motorcycle riders, and, still later, the hot rodders and the sports car buffs.

For many young men in New England, the drudgery of farming the rocky soil had less appeal than the high adventure of going to sea; so it was that many of them drifted to the ports and became seamen. Even lads of ten or twelve sometimes were signed on to learn seafaring. There were fishing vessels that went off to the banks and might be gone only a few weeks on each cruise. But there were other vessels, the larger ones in the foreign trade, which might be away from the home port for a year or more.

In the course of one of these lengthier voyages, the young man fresh off the farm would visit exotic lands, see strange sights, and mingle with aliens whose looks, language, and behavior were unlike anything he had ever imagined at home. Going to sea thus was a broadening educational experience.

For a great many New Englanders just growing into manhood, it was an experience that taught them to see things in a different light, to be tolerant of alien people and ideas, and even to be skeptical of the powerful dogma being preached at home by Puritan divines. In this way the lure of the sea became a contributing factor in opening the eyes of youthful New Englanders and undermining the rigidities of Puritan intolerance.

Never on Sunday

Elaborate precautions were taken to protect the purity and orthodoxy of the infant Puritan colony. Only church members could elect the community leaders – and church membership was rigorously controlled – but attendance at church services was mandatory for every resident whether a member of the church or not. Ministers of the church faced sharp scrutiny; they were booted out of the colony unceremoniously if they displayed any signs of deviating from purest Puritanism.

Sunday was the day when the piety of the community touched its zenith and when the grimness of the Puritan lives was most acute. All work was prohibited on the Sabbath. A man couldn't cut any firewood or patch a roof; a woman couldn't sew a seam, sweep her kitchen floor, or light a fire under the soup kettle.

Nor could there be any hilarity, gaming or play on Sunday. Anyone caught running, jumping, or singing was fined. The New Haven colony was especially strict. It penalized parishioners caught violating the Sabbath by shaving, making up beds, or kissing one's own children. (There was, or course, a permanent ban seven days a week against dancing or card–playing.)

Sunday's routine began early in the morning with the call to meeting. Until church bells could be acquired and installed, the call to meeting was sounded with a gun shot, a horn blast, or a drum roll. Families then assembled at the meeting house and took their places on the wooden benches.

36

A standard sermon ran for two hours. If a minister felt particularly inspired and got into high gear he might carry on for four hours. As a warm-up for this mighty sermon, the parishioners were led in a lengthy prayer, which could drag on for an hour, then participated in what was called "a lining of the psalms." A deacon would read a line from the psalms, then the congregation would repeat it, droning in unison. There was no music during the service.

All this transpired at the morning service. At mid-day a break was taken so parishioners could partake of the food prepared the day before. (Cooking on the Sabbath was forbidden.) Then after the mid-day break, the parishioners returned to their benches for the afternoon service. This was a duplicate of the one in the morning, with another one of those two-hour-plus sermons.

It made for a long and tiring experience. But nobody was permitted to catnap during the service. A "tithingman" with a long pole saw to that. One end of his pole had a knob; to the other end was attached a feather. If this functionary caught a parishioner nodding, he would reach out his pole and touch the nodder, using either the knob end or the feather end as circumstances seemed to require.

No heat was provided in the early meeting houses, thus making the Sunday services even more of an ordeal in frigid weather. Mr. Adams, the historian, has concluded that "a modern barn (in 1890) would be more comfortable than the meeting houses" in which his colonial ancestors worshipped.

Puritan parsons laid it on the line with utmost vigor and didn't mince any words. The typical fire and brimstone sermon style is illustrated in this sample delivered in the early 1630's by the Rev. Thomas Shepard:

Every natural man is born full of sin, as full as a toad is of poison, as full as ever his skin can hold; mind, will, eyes, mouth, every limb of his body and every piece of his soul is full of sin. Thy heart is a foul sink of atheism, sodomy, blasphemy, murder, whoredom, adultery, witchcraft, buggery; so that if thou hast any good thing in thee, it is but as a drop of rose water in a bowl of poison. Thou feelest not all of these things stirring within thee at one time, but they are in thee like a nest of snakes in an old hedge.

One can assume that Mr. Shepard resorted to appropriate gestures to drive home the points in his stirring message.

Some parsons had a better grasp of scary metaphors or a

more forceful way of presenting the Holy word. But if the parson was worth his salt he was expected to be able to stretch out his fiery tirades to the acceptable two-hour length and draw a frightening picture calculated to strake terror into the hearts of the wayward. One of the most admired ministers was the Rev. Jonathan Edwards of Connecticut. He won wide acclaim for his colorful and effective style:

The God that holds you over the pit of hell, much as anyone holds some loathesome insect over the flame, abhors you and is dreadfully provoked. His wrath toward you burns like fire.

A couple hours of this in Mr. Edwards' little church invariably provoked weeping, wailing, and sudden repentance among the minister's shaken listeners.

A Mouse and a Snake

The constant presence of supernatural forces was a basic theme in Puritan theology. God and the devil always were close at hand and every event could be ascribed to one or the other. If a lightning bolt should strike a tree and topple it across a path, that might be interpreted as the work of the devil, or it might be interpreted as the work of God to test the courage and steadfastness of the people. Ministers often spent days arguing whether a given happening was the handiwork of God or of the devil.

An unusual occurence at Watertown, Massachusetts, in 1632 stirred widespread interest. Witnesses reported that a mouse, just an ordinary mouse, and a snake, just an ordinary snake, became engaged in a desperate struggle. A crowd gathered. The onlookers were fascinated by the strange combat, and they were greatly puzzled when, after a lengthy battle, the mouse prevailed and killed the snake.

The witnesses did not know what this meant, but being Godly people they were certain it must be some kind of a supernatural manifestation. So they took the matter to the Rev. John Wilson, "a sincere and holy man" who was then pastor of the church at Boston.

Mr. Wilson heard the evidence then went into a deep period of contemplation. Finally he emerged with a decision. It was a decision which pleased the witnesses and, when spread across the colony, caused much satisfaction.

"The snake was the devil," Mr. Wilson decided, "and the mouse was a poor, contemptible people which God had brought hither, which should overcome Satan here, and dispossess Satan of his kingdom."

After that striking demonstration the colonists had heightened confidence that God was on their side. They were proud of this additional proof that they were the "contemptible people" chosen by God to carry His word into the American wilderness. And they were strengthened in their conviction that they would overcome their many difficulties and prevail over Satan just as that little mouse had prevailed over the snake.

Fanatics in Power

The religious fervor that so dominated life in colonial New England was a common feature of the time. A similar fervor was dominant throughout Europe. In each place spiritual leaders who had achieved power and influence became convinced that they had found and had embraced the only true faith. Once they reached that point, they felt impelled to hunt down and persecute anyone who disagreed with their dogmas and rejected their prejudices.

Down through the centuries the fanatical zeal of religious leaders has led to many of history's most blood-thirsty episodes: the Crusades against the infidels in the Eleventh Century, the Roman persecution of the early Christians, the torture inflicted on the Huguenots in France, and the horrendous practices during the Spanish Inquisition.

Witchcraft, an accepted phenomenon among the early pagans, fell into disrepute as Christianity spread its message through the Medieval world. Christian leaders regarded all forms of witchcraft and sorcery as Satanic evils threatening Christian belief. Beginning around 1450 and continuing for some two hundred and fifty years, Christian fanatics waged fierce campaigns against witches and wizards. Suspects were rounded up in droves. Confessions were extorted. Thousands were executed, often by burning at the stake.

The mania spread to the New World where "witches" were identified and persecuted in Massachusetts, Connecticut, and Virginia. The craze reached alarming proportions in Salem,

Massachusetts, where a score of persons were hanged in 1692.

Though the fervor has diminished in modern times, it has not vanished. Religious fanaticism has created the terrorist bedlam in Iran and the senseless, long-drawn-out fighting and killing in Ireland.

Religious Freedom?

The Puritans often spoke of religious freedom. They had been oppressed in England, often ridiculed or punished for their religious views, and they persuaded themselves that they had migrated to America largely to find a place where they could practice and enjoy their religious freedom. That is what they may have thought. But the reality is quite different. These Puritans were not seeking religious freedom as we understand that term because that would have meant freedom for each individual to worship in his own way. That kind of individual freedom had no place at all in the Puritan community.

What the Puritans really wanted was religious isolation. They wanted a wall around their community to protect the good people inside from the heretics and other agents of Satan who were outside. The wall often was referred to as a hedge and it figured prominently in many a rousing Puritan sermon.

In this comfortable isolation every member of the Godly community would worship in the same way, accept the same dogmas, abide by the same communal rules. There was no room at all for toleration of different beliefs or for individual liberty of conscience. Indeed, such things were regarded as monstrous evils. Whenever they were mentioned, the Puritan parsons were quick to strike them down as sinful.

The Rev. John Norton denounced the toleration of other sects as the "liberty to blaspheme, to seduce others from the living God, to tell lies in the name of God."

The Rev. Increase Mather deplored "the hideous clamor for liberty of conscience."

The Rev. Urian Oakes warned his parishioners that the toleration of non-Puritan opinions was "the first-born of abominations."

In some intellectual circles of Europe at this time the idea of democracy was being discussed. Puritan leaders made short shift of this radical notion. It simply didn't square with their idea of a proper government.

The Rev. John Cotton couched it in these terms:

*I cannot conceive that ever God did ordeyn democracy as
a fitt government eyther for church or commonwealth. If
the people be governors, who shall be governed?*

The Puritans were not always consistent. As an example,
before the migration to America one of their strongest complaints against the Anglican Church was that it had become
dominated by the state. They objected strenuously to a system in which the government appointed bishops and otherwise
forced its pattern of religion upon the people. And yet, once
the Puritans reached America and got established, they set up
their own church-state authority which was just as coercive,
just as authoritarian, and just as ruthless as the one they had
criticized so vehemently in England.

Thus what we find in New England is a narrow Puritan path
with no allowance for the slightest deviation. The crusty
Puritans were certain of their own righteousness, equally certain that anyone who differed from them was ignorant of God's
way and probably influencd by demonic forces.

Toleration would begin to seep in much later, as we shall
see, but for the first half century or so the communities in
New England were dominated by sanctimonious bigots.

Puritan Bigots

Bigotry is one of the unfortunate constants of history. It
has been a feature of every society since time began, and it
was particularly widespread in the Seventeenth Century. Dissidents were burned at the stake in Spain. Protestant
Huguenots were tortured in France. Roman Catholics were
persecuted in England. Jews had been victimized in many
lands for centuries. Thus the bigotry we find in colonial New
England was part of a common tapestry that had spread across
the civilized world.

Other colonies in a young America were familiar with
bigotry. In Virginia it often was a social bigotry based on
class distinctions. In New Amsterdam the Dutch tended to be
broadly tolerant of strangers, but on occasion when in their
cups the Dutch burghers could work up a fine head of bigoted
steam against individuals whose race, color, faith, or language displeased them.

Nowhere else, however, did blatant religious bigotry reach
such heights of viciousness as it did in Puritan New England.
A fierce and unyielding bigotry dominated Puritan lives.
These colonists held in contempt anyone who didn't worship

exactly as they worshipped, and they were venomous in persecuting anyone who dared to question their faith. Heretics were fined, jailed, whipped, or banished. Some were hanged.

Bigotry permeated the colony. It seeped into every aspect of people's lives. It was a trait so deeply rooted in the Puritan character that it seemed to have achieved a degree of permanence.

But it was not permanent. Indeed, what makes the New England bigotry most unusual is the speed with which it burned itself out. In roughly a single century - barely an eyeblink in historical terms - the flame was gone and only the embers remained. It was as though a pendulum had swung. The intolerance of Puritan New England in the Seventeenth Century changed to the tolerance of the Eighteenth Century when the descendants of those bigoted Puritans laid aside the intolerance of their ancestors. A new generation - including John Adams, Ben Franklin, Elbridge Gerry, John Hancock, and others - found common cause with Thomas Jefferson and James Madison in shaping a Declaration, a Constitution and a nation in which toleration was a guiding principle.

The Quakers Persecuted

In their climate of raw bigotry, the Puritans developed a particular contempt for the Quakers. Oh, they looked with scorn on the Jews, and they despised the Moslems, the Roman Catholics, the Anglicans, and any others whose practices didn't conform to Puritan doctrine but they reserved their most savage condemnation for the members of the Society of Friends, better known as Quakers.

From a theological view this is strange because the Puritans and the Quakers agreed on many doctrinal points. Both were Christian and Protestant. Both shunned the pomp and ceremony they saw in the Catholic Church and the Church of England. Both put a high value on morality, goodness, hard work, and obedience. Both believed in punishment for sinners and their lists of sins were similar.

All this being so, one would have expected the Puritans to accept the fellowship of the Quakers. But that did not happen. What developed was hatred, not fellowship. The colonial records are littered with instances in which the Puritans inflicted harsh penalties on miscreants who "confessed to being Quakers." There are a great many of these "confessions" in the record - so many, in fact, that one is led to suspect the Puritans may have used strong measures to obtain them. After all, the torture of prisoners was an accepted practice almost everywhere in the Seventeenth Century.

Some Quakers got off lightly with a fine or a brief sentence. Others were put in the stocks, tied to a post and lashed, or banished from the community. At least three Quakers were hanged.

In other parts of the world at this time some societies still burned prisoners at the stake as an extreme form of punishment. This is one penalty the Puritans did not apply. Though they did authorize lashings and an occasional hanging, there is no evidence that they ever resorted to burning at the stake.

Among the Puritans the prevailing opinion was that the Quakers were folks with strange practices whose presence was not welcome in the Puritan community. If the Quakers would just stay away and mind their own business elsewhere, fine: the Puritans would leave them alone if they kept their distance. But the pesky Quakers kept returning. They seemed to hunger for martyrdom and they persisted in trickling into the Puritan villages in ones and twos and threes as though in a deliberate plan to irritate, antagonize, and otherwise disrupt the peace and harmony of Puritan society. For the Puritans, this was intolerable behavior.

In 1658 the Quaker problem was brought up at a session of the New England Confederation. This was the regional federation formed earlier to help the various colonies tackle common problems. At the meeting in September, 1658, the Confederation agreed on a procedure for handling the Quaker annoyance. The procedure had three steps. The first time a Quaker showed up in a Puritan colony he would be banished. If he showed up a second time, he would be "maimed and banished." (The colonies had various forms of maiming as punishment. The list included a brand on cheek or hand, burning a hole in the ear, or burning a hole in the tongue. Inventive judges or bailiffs sometimes dreamed up other forms of maiming to add to the list.) Finally, the confederation agreed that if a Quaker should return to a Puritan community a third time he would be put to death. Enough was enough.

Why were the Quakers singled out for such persecution? It was largely because the Quakers were stubbornly and persistently obstreperous. Some Catholics and other non-Puritans entered the Puritan settlements from time to time. If they did not flaunt their differences and if they accepted the Puritan rules they were pretty much left alone. But the Quakers deliberately spurned Puritan rules. They refused to attend Puritan church services and they refused to pay taxes to support that church.

Nor is that all for there were other Quaker practices that wrankled the Puritans. The Quakers did not accept ministers, for instance, believing that no middle man was necessary between man and God. And the Quakers refused to doff their hats to superiors – as the Puritans did – on the ground that all men were created equal and there weren't any "superiors" walking around. For such behavior the Quakers were branded heretics in the Puritan community. Punishment was automatic.

The Quakers generally were quiet, orderly, peaceable people. They went about their business with a patient diligence, accepting the persecution with good grace. Occasionally, however, the bitter hostility they faced in the Puritan communities caused them to react in anger. A Quaker burst into a meeting at Cambridge, Massachusetts, one Sunday, crashed two bottles together and standing amid the shattered glass shouted out: "Thus will the Lord break you in pieces!" He was jailed.

On another memorable occasion, a Quaker woman removed her clothing and marched stark naked into a meeting at Newbury, Massachusetts. She did this, she explained, "to show the people the nakedness of their rulers." The people somehow failed to get the point and the woman was banished.

In some of the other colonies – Rhode Island and Pennsylvania are examples – the Quakers found a congenial environment and friendly neighbors, but in Puritan New England they were always regarded as undesirable aliens.

44

Nicholas Upsall's Scheme

The case of Nicholas Upsall tells us something significant about prevailing conditions. For many years Mr. Upsall operated a taproom in Boston known as the Red Lyon Inn. He had come over in 1630 on the *Mary and John,* had become a freeman, had obtained his license to run the inn, and in every way could be described as a good citizen and a pillar in the community.

One day in 1656 the word reached his taproom that two women, Mary Fisher and Ann Austen, had just arrived on a ship from England, had been identified as Quakers and had been slapped into jail. This news did not bother Mr. Upsall. Quakers were showing up regularly in the community and just as regularly were being jailed. It was a common occurence.

But a few days later a more disturbing rumor circulated in the taproom. Mr. Upsall heard that the authorities had decided to get rid of these Quaker women by starving them to death. No food was to be provided for them at their jail. Mr. Upsall made some inquiries and learned that the rumor was true. A deliberate decision had been made to starve these two prisoners.

This was too much. Mr. Upsall's conscience didn't permit him to ignore this decision. So he pulled a few strings, got in touch with the jailer, and arranged to pay the jailer five shillings a week as a bribe to sneak food in to the two Quaker women.

Somehow the authorities got wind of Mr. Upsall's scheme. The compassionate taproom proprietor was arrested, brought to court, fined L20 (a large sum in those days), and banished from the colony. Winter was coming on and Mr. Upsall was ill-equipped to fend for himself in the wild. He might have perished in the forest had it not been for some friendly Indians who took him in. They fed him, then escorted him safely down the coast to sanctuary in Plymouth.

Three years later the authorities at Boston softened their position and permitted Mr. Upsall to leave Plymouth and move in with his brother-in-law in Boston. But the authorities were alert for hanky-panky, so they put a strict proviso in their ruling. Mr. Upsall could make the move back to Boston, they decided, "provided he did not corrupt anybody with his pernicious opinions nor teache the diabolical doctrines and horrid tenets of the cursed sect of Quakers."

The record does not tell us what happened to the two Quaker women who had been consigned to death by starvation. They may have been shipped back to England.

Toleration Appears

Not many years were to pass in the New World before the Puritans realized that their stern views of orderly community life were being undermined.

For one thing, the flood of immigrants pouring into the colonies included many non-Puritans. There were folks professing all sorts of outlandish faiths. There were Germans, Swedes, Danes, Irish Catholics, Dutch Protestants, French Huguenots, Scottish Presbyterians, and Jews from various parts of Europe. Only a few of these aliens could be absorbed in the Puritan community without radically changing the community's character. But there were so many of them!

In the year 1630 alone, one thousand seven hundred new-comers settled in the Massachusetts Bay colony. Thereafter for the next dozen years more than one thousand additional immigrants arrived each year. English Protestants still dominated the population numerically by a wide margin. But the various minority groups were becoming increasingly visible factors and some accommodation became necessary.

Also, because of the enormous spread of open land in the New World, a settler who did not like his circumstances or his neighborhood could trudge off into the wilderness and either find a community more to his taste or simply build himself a cabin in the wilds. Many of them did just that.

The Puritan leaders, early on, recognized this peril of dispersal. A widely-dispersed colony would be difficult to control. In an effort to prevent too much scattering and to keep their communities firmly contained and under a tight rein, the Puritans adoped a law that no man could build a home more than a mile from a church - and no new church could be erected without approval of the authorities. This was an earnest try, but it was one of the first Puritan rules to be abandoned. It simply didn't work.

Circumstances also forced the Puritans to scuttle their cherished belief in a church-state theocracy. For decades only church members could cast votes in community affairs. However, this qualification was dropped in 1691 when a new charter for Massachusetts was adopted: the new charter established the voting right for every man who owned property, with no regard whatever for religious affiliation.

The net effect of all this was that no matter how desperately the Puritan stalwarts tried to hold their line and protect their ideology, they were being forced to adjust to changing circumstances. That adjustment inevitably meant some loosening of the Puritan strictures and a corresponding loosening of the rigid Puritan intolerance.

Far-reaching changes occurred in the colonies as the people put down roots and their communities matured. During the first half century or so in New England – say from 1630 to 1680 – the colonies took on an entirely different look and character. Homes became more substantial and comfortable. Farming and fishing became more efficient. Mercantile trading flourished. Simple manufactures were started. The colonists ate better, dressed better, and by 1680 faced fewer of the perils that dogged earlier settlers.

Of all the changes, however, the most momentous, the one that would have the most significant effect on the new nation in America, was the appearance of toleration.

We cannot say precisely where or when toleration first appeared in the colonies. It simply crept in gradually at many different places, at many different times, and from many different directions. It seeped into the lives of the colonists so gradually that most of them were not even aware of any change. But once started, the progress of toleration was inexorable.

In the beginning, as we have noted, toleration ranked high on the list of Puritan sins. Puritan parsons in the 1630's regarded it as a flagrant evil. They condemned all non-Puritans as pagans or agents of Satan, and they despised anyone who refused to worship exactly as they worshipped. There wasn't any place in their make-up for even a smidgen of tolerance toward those who professed other faiths. The worst of the lot on the Puritan list were the Quakers. And how those Puritan preachers enjoyed their emotional tirades against "the diabolical doctrines of the cursed sect of Quakers." Yet, for all the venom the preachers ladled over the Quakers, they had plenty in reserve to spread over the Catholics, the Jews, the Baptists, and those others who rejected Puritan dogma.

John Winthrop at first embraced this narrow view toward other sects. Indeed, his original blueprint for the colony in America called for what he described as a "spiritual aristocracy." He proposed that a small group of his fellow emigrants in 1630, a group including only the most pious, the wealthiest and the better educated, be established as the ruling authority. This exclusive little clique of leaders would set the rules, administer the laws, collect the taxes – in fact, run the whole shebang. It would have been a pure oligarchy, a government ruled by a select few.

Winthrop was persuaded by his friends, however, that this would be too narrow and selective for a proper administration.

So a compromise was worked out. Under the compromise, all members of the church, not just a handful of aristocrats, would be permitted to vote on community affairs.

Could anyone join the church and thus get the right to vote? No. Church membership was rigidly controlled by the church leadership. Everyone in the community had to attend church, true enough, and stiff fines were assessed on those who failed to show up for services, but to become a member of the church one had to pass muster before a gimlet-eyed and deeply suspicious little band of bigoted church leaders. Thus was the purity of the church maintained. And thus was the community protected from the sinfullness the leaders imagined was rampant in the outside world.

Up to this point, church and state were joined as a single administrative unit. That was part of the Puritans' natural order. In fact, it was the way governments were operating throughout the civilized world (probably also in the uncivilized world) in the Seventeenth Century. It was customary for a monarch to decide which religious faith to accept, and whatever the monarch chose automatically became the nation's official state religion. Each loyal subject was expected to follow the monarch's lead and embrace the state religion.

Much later, as an offshoot to the growth of toleration, the colonists would begin to consider, admire, and finally accept the revolutionary idea of separating church and state. But it did not come swiftly or easily. In fact, it started only as a wildly radical notion. Gradually it achieved some standing and began to be examined seriously.

The colonies of Rhode Island, New Jersey, Delaware, and Pennsylvania were the first ones to accept the complete separation of church and state. Following their lead, the Founding Fathers wrote church-state separation into the Constitution of the new nation. By the end of the first quarter of the Nineteenth Century there were no state-supported churches anywhere in the United States. The only concession granted to churches from that time on was the tax exemption for religious edifices.

England imposed the death penalty for adultery in the early 1600's, and the Puritans carried this penalty with them into America. In the course of time, though, the Puritans amended the penalty. First, they dropped the death penalty and substituted a branding of the culprit. Still later, they dropped the branding and merely required the culprit to wear a prominently-displayed scarlet letter, the letter "A".

Many other laws and practices brought over by the

colonists underwent changes (revision or abandonment) in the New World. This was due partly to conditions in America and partly to the gradual change in beliefs that occurs naturally with the passage of time. As an example, England observed a law of primogeniture. That law meant, simply, that the oldest son inherited his father's entire estate; younger sons and all the daughters had no legal inheritance whatever. The Puritans in New England ignored this law from the start. The English class system did hang on for a while in America, but it, too, was forced to give way gradually as the years rolled by.

Meanwhile, streaks of compassion began to appear occasionally in the Puritan communities where compassion, generally, was a rarity in the early years.

Not long after the settlement was established at Boston, a law was enacted against cruelty to animals. (This in a community which still hanged adulterers.) Possibly the Puritans were moved by the Biblical injunction that a merciful man must be merciful to his beast. In any case, the law was enacted. It provided:

No man shall exercise any tiranny or cruelty toward any bruit creatures usually kept for man's use.

Strange, too, but also compassionate, was the early Puritan attitude toward the welfare of children.

The town fathers in Cambridge at one point decided that a man named Francis Bale had too many children. The decision was reached that Mr. Bale and his wife were unable to provide proper care for their large brood. So the town fathers decided that Mr. and Mrs. Bales must give up two of their youngsters. Mrs. Bale apparently raised an objection to the ruling. The court record reads as follows:

The town advised him (Mr. Bale) to dispose of two of his children. His wife was not willing, and they p'swaded him to p'swade his wife to it.

That phrase "dispose of" did not mean what it might be taken to mean in this day and age. In colonial times, it meant simply that the surplus children would be farmed out to another family better able to give them proper care. This was a customary solution for the problem in that period.

On several occasions courageous citizens dared to follow their own consciences rather than bow to Puritan dictates. The case of Nicholas Upsall, who flouted the authorities' plan to starve two Quaker women, is one example.

A comparable incident of individual conscience occurred in New Haven, Connecticut. One of the standard practices in that community was to tie up convicted prostitutes in the public square and apply the lash. New Haven didn't mess around with sinners. It followed a moral code that probably was stricter than the codes in any other Puritan community and it was firm in meting out punishment. There came a day when a prostitute was tied up and prepared for a flogging. But the public whipper delegated to carry out the sentence suddenly decided that he would not go through with it. He put down his whip and announced that he would rather pay a fine for shirking his duty. Since nobody else would take on the flogging chore, the woman went unflogged and was set free. We cannot measure just how far the effects of this incident carried.

It shows on the record, though, that the flogging of prisoners gradually vanished from the penal systems in America.

Puritan Violence

The Puritans didn't shrink from violence if it served their purpose. A Scotch-Irish group of thirty immigrant families moved west of Boston and settled in a backwoods area near the present site of Worcester. There they built a Presbyterian church. When word of this spread, angry Yankee Puritans formed a posse, marched on the church, tore it down and set fire to the pieces. So much for the Presbyterians.

A bloodier display occurred in 1655 at what is now Annapolis, Maryland. A colony of Puritans had settled earlier along Chesapeake Bay in Virginia, while the Annapolis area was settled by a group of colonists acting for Cecil Calvert, the second Lord Baltimore; this group included many Catholics. After a spell, the Puritans found fault with their location so they decided to move north and occupy the more attractive Annapolis area. The fact that an established colony already was there did not bother the Puritans. They simply pushed in. A brief period of fighting ensued during which the invaders routed the non-Puritan colonists. To celebrate their victory, the invading Puritans hanged a few of their more prominent prisoners, expelled the local Jesuits, and passed a batch of stiff anti-Catholic laws. So much for the Papists and their supporters.

Despite all their preaching and praying and their superficial aura of moral perfection, the Puritan communities were by no means free of criminal activity. It might even be argued that the Puritan towns had more anti-social sinners than did other towns which laid less stress on surface righteousness. In any case, the record suggests that the Puritans devoted an inordinate amount of their time enacting and enforcing laws against crime, then catching and punishing their rascals.

The English criminal code of the early Sixteenth Century was the code the Puritan emigrants brought along with them as part of their baggage from the homeland. It was a rigorous code. It provided the death penalty for murder, treason, piracy, adultery, rape, and a variety of minor offenses down to the theft of any property valued at more than a shilling.

A most peculiar feature of the code was called "benefit of clergy." Originally this was an arrangement to exempt clergymen from punishment in civil courts – the assumption being that the church could handle such matters exclusively in the church's own courts. As time ran on, however, "benefit of clergy" became a legal gimmick that accommodated the prejudice of social class. Members of the lower class were routinely punished for their crimes. But members of the upper class were treated differently. They often were covered by the provision for "benefit of clergy" and thus might escape punishment for their misbehavior.

Under the "benefit of clergy" procedure, a reading test was applied. The alleged criminal was ordered to read aloud a chapter from the Bible. If he was a lower-class illiterate, he would fail the test and face punishment. But if he was from the upper class, a person with some education and the ability to read, he would read the Bible chapter, pass the test, and be freed from the charge on the ground that his proven ability to read gave him the "benefit of clergy."

Anybody smart enough to read was assumed to have reached a higher educational and moral level on a par with members of the clergy. And those who had attained this lofty height were assumed to have acquired also a measure of wisdom which made them exempt from punishment for ordinary crime. It is hard for us to understand such a ridiculous system, yet with a few modifications that is the system that prevailed for many years.

The individual colonies often revised the basic English code to suit their community's preference. Thus the settlement at Windsor, Connecticut, in 1640 imposed the death penalty for adultery, rape, witchcraft, kidnaping, and "worship of any but the true God."

For reasons lost in the mists of time, the General Court of Connecticut in 1641 decided that lying was an offense that

51

required some special attention. The Court, therefore, assigned Mr. Webster of Hartford and Mr. Phelps of Windsor to consult with the elders of their churches and prepare instructions for the Court on a proper punishment for lying.

This matter apparently was set aside and allowed to simmer for quite a while. It finally cropped up in 1650 when the Connecticut General Court adopted a lengthy list of crimes and appropriate punishments. The list included:

-- Lying by anyone over age 14. Punishable by fines, stocks, or stripes.

-- Absence from church. Fine of five shillings.

-- Forgery. Three days in pillory.

-- Fornication. Fine, whipping or prohibition to marry.

-- Burglary. Punished by branding "B" on hand.

-- Open contempt for God, for the minister, or for the church. First offense: reproof. Second offense: fine of five pounds and standing in the pillory on a lecture day, bearing on the breast a paper duly labelled in capital letters "An Obstinate and Open Contemner of God's Holy Word."

Morality in Windsor

The community of Windsor, Connecticut, was particularly diligent in upholding the moral code and punishing its sinners.

Consider the case in the late 1640's when an unmarried young woman in Windsor became pregnant and gave birth. An investigation was made and three young men were brought into court. Two of them were sentenced "to stand upon the pillory from the ringing of the first bell to the end of the lecture, then to be whipped at the cart's tail and to be whipped in like manner in Windsor on eight days following."

The third young culprit got sterner punishment. In addition to the whippings, the court ordered that the letter "R" be burned on his cheek and that he be forced to pay the girl's parents £10. The court seemingly found this third culprit the likely father of the bastard child, though how this was determined at a time when blood tests were unknown we can only guess. The General Court completed this incident by instructing two citizens in good standing "to see that some punishment is inflicted on the girl for concealing it so long."

On several unpleasant occasions the Puritans learned that some of their ministers were not quite as sanctimoniously righteous and free of sin as they pretended to be.

The Rev. John Cotton, son of the Bay colony's most

eminent prelate, John Cotton, also a Reverand, was found guilty of adultery. The younger minister was dismissed from his church in disgrace. As further punishment he was ordered to journey to South Carolina and serve as minister for a new Puritan community there. It was a form of exile from the "Eden" in Massachusetts, though the South Carolinians may have viewed it differently.

Another respected minister in the Bay colony married a wealthy widow. Then, to the vast embarrassment of the parish, it was discovered that this parson had another wife back in England.

Unusual, too, was the case of the Rev. Stephen Batchellor, an 80-year-old minister of a flock in New Hampshire. The elderly Mr. Batchellor was convicted of the charge that "he did solicit the chastity of his neighbor's wife." As punishment, the court barred him from the pulpit for two years. At the end of the two years he was reinstated, presumably on the ground that he now was old enough to know better.

As time ran on, the New England Puritans eased many of the restrictions they had imposed on themselves. But on one aspect of the social life, drinking, the Puritans moved in the opposite direction, toward stiffer restrictions.

In the beginning the colonists imbibed freely, mostly on wine, beer, and hard cider. The Bible assured them that these liquids could be considered "good creatures of God." That Biblical injunction was sufficient to justify.

After a few years, however, Governor Winthrop was sorely distraught when he noticed that drunkenness had become a serious problem in the community. At the governor's direction, the General Court passed new restrictions on the use of alcoholic beverages. As an explanation, the court declared that over-indulgence had become "an inducement to drunkenness and occasions of quarreling and bloodshed and much waste of wine and beer, and vexing to master and mistress of the feast, forced thereby to drink more oft than they would."

From that point on, drunkenness, once largely ignored, became a sin and all the Puritan colonies imposed stiff punishment on the imbibing sinners.

A Dutchman visiting Hartford in the mid-1600's was surprised to find the harsh penalties being meted out there to drunkards. "Whoever drinks himself drunk," this visitor wrote, "they tie to a post and whip him as they do thieves in Holland."

* * * * *

At the start the New England colonies shunned tolerance as a despicable evil. They nourished a conviction of their own righteousness and a furious contempt for non-Puritans but as the years rolled by, toleration began to creep in. The force of the Puritans' convictions became tempered by reality and experience. They began to suspect, bit by bit, that they might not be the exclusive repositories of goodness and that their non-Puritan neighbors might not be merely blasphemous tools of Satan. In short, intolerance gave way, inch by inch. And as it faded, the way was paved for more sympathetic leaders who, a centur later, would devise a Declaration and a Constitution which would stand as models for tolerance, for justice, and for better government.

CHAPTER THREE

INDIAN AND EUROPEAN NEIGHBORS

Indian Friends and Foes

A couple of erroneous notions about the American Indians were common in England in the early 1600's. Most of the Puritan migrants subscribed to one or the other.

One notion held that the American Indians were like children: innocent, unschooled, ignorant, and malleable. Those Puritans who happened to be steeped in missionary zeal, as many were, vowed to carry the word of Jesus into the American wilderness and convert these pagan Indians into Christians. It was viewed as an exciting challenge, an enterprise these pious and willing servants of God were eager to take on.

The other notion, which many colonists feared was the fact, labeled all the Indians as cunning and dangerous agents of Satan. The Puritans held out little hope that the forces of Satan could be put to rout; they believed there was little chance that the Indians could be exorcised and brought safely into the Christian fold. Among the Puritans who subscribed to this notion, the feeling was that the colonists must be ever watchful. They must be suspicious of the natives at every turn and always alert for demonic Indian tricks. Out of this fear and suspicion grew another thought, namely, that the only good Indian was a dead Indian.

Both of these notions were flawed. They were flawed chiefly because they assumed all the Indians could be lumped into a single convenient category. In one version all the Indians were innocent and childlike; in the other all were vicious agents of Satan. The reality was, however, that the Indians didn't fit so neatly into any single category. They were simply too numerous and too different to conform to any single pattern.

The total population of Indians north of Mexico in the 1600's has been estimated roughly at one million. They were scattered among scores of tribes and sub-tribes. Some were nomads. Others had established settlements and dabbled in agriculture. A few Indian tribes had dogs, but there were no other domestic animals. Some of the tribes collaborated with one another in friendly fashion. Others were fiercely antagonistic and constantly feuding.

The most striking differences among the Indians, however, were in their intelligence, their character, their behavior, and their attitude toward the invading white men. The plain fact is that some Indians were bright and some were stupid. Some were amiable and some were hostile. Some were openly kind and generous to the colonists; others were sly, crafty, and given to thievery, treachery, and horrendous cruelty. In short, it was a remarkably diverse population. There simply was no common trait of character or behavior that could be applied accurately to all the Indians in America.

Encounter at Plymouth

The Pilgrims who landed at Plymouth in 1620 were fortunate in their first encounter with the Indians. An epidemic had swept through that area and had wiped out most of the natives. The precise nature of this epidemic has never been determined. One supposition is that it may have been a disease introduced by European explorers. It could have been small pox. Or it could have been some illness which was common and relatively harmless for the Europeans, but which was lethal for the Indians who had not developed any immunity.

All through that first bleak winter at Plymouth, the colonists saw no Indians nor any signs that Indians might be about.

On a sunny day in the spring of 1621, however, the colonists were startled when a lone Indian emerged from the forest and sauntered into their village. Mothers hastily shooed their children to shelter. The men reached for their guns.

But the visitor soon allayed their fears. He wore a broad smile, showed the palm of his hand in a friendly gesture, and to the vast astonishment of the villagers, spoke in English. It wasn't fluent English and conversation was a bit awkward; nevertheless, with a few basic words and many gestures the Indian visitor explained that his name was Samoset, that he came from the "east" (perhaps the coast of what is now Maine and Canada) and that he had learned his English words from sailors and fishermen who frequented that area.

Gov. William Bradford of the Plymouth colony – adopting the guise of a non-participating reporter – has described the meeting this way:

> Samoset spoke to them in broken English, which they could well understand, but marveled at it. At length they understood by discourse with him that he was not of these parts, but belonged to the eastern parts where some English ships came to fish. He (Samoset) became profitable to them (the Pilgrims) in acquainting them with many things...He told them of another Indian whose name was Squanto, a native of this place, who had been in England and could speak English better than himself.

Sure enough, a few days later Samoset returned bringing with him the other Indian, Squanto. The Pilgrims gave gifts to Samoset, thanked him for his kindness, and he went on his way.

But Squanto stayed on in Plymouth. He was a lonely, homeless orphan, apparently the only survivor of the disease that had wiped out his tribe, and he was as pleased to settle in this village of white men as the villagers were to have him. (The evidence suggests that some early explorer kidnaped Squanto and took him to England where the captive learned his English. Just how or when he got back to America has not been determined.)

Squanto became an important person in Plymouth. He taught the Pilgrims how to hunt, fish, and grow corn and beans. Most of the colonists were helplessly inexperienced in these basic activities and Squanto's lessons were vital. Indeed, if it had not been for his help it's a question whether the little colony could have survived.

The Puritan colonists at Massachusetts Bay similarly had agreeable first encounters with the Indians. During the critical first months in 1630 when the colonists were short of food and facing starvation, the Indians brought in baskets of corn to help – as Roger Clap described earlier.

Later on, when the Puritan leaders found it necessary to banish individuals who had violated their stern laws, the culprits sometimes were shipped back to England, but on occasion were simply driven into exile in the forest. Indians often found these exiles, fed them, gave them shelter, and sometimes escorted them to the more tolerant white community down the coast at Plymouth. Roger Williams had this

experience after he was banished from Boston.   Nicholas Upsall, the pub proprietor who tried to save the lives of two
Quaker women, also was taken in by Indians.

The Pequot War

The amiable first encounters with Indians at Plymouth and
at Massachusetts Bay represent one side of the coin – the
pleasant side. On the other side of that coin, unfortunately, is
the unpleasant fact that some of the Indians some of the time
were prone to hostility, villainy, and the most unspeakable
crimes.

In 1637 the Pequots went on the warpath. Their lodgings
were chiefly along the shore of what is now Connecticut, and
for some time they had chafed uneasily as they saw the white
men pressing settlements deeper and deeper into what had
been exclusive Pequot territory. The bitterness finally came
to a head and the Pequots went on a rampage. They swept into
colonial habitations, stealing cattle, burning dwellings, and
torturing and murdering the colonists.

From the besieged settlement at Saybrook, John Higginson
sent out a plaintive call for help from the other colonies. "The
eyes of all the Indians in the countrey are upon the English,"
he wrote. "If some speedie course be not taken to tame the
pride of these now insulting Pequots we are like to have all
the Indians in the countrey about our ears." There wasn't
much exaggeration in Higginson's plea. The peril was real,
especially for the settlements along the Connecticut River and
along the Sound.

In response, leaders in Boston and Plymouth, Massachusetts, Rhode Island, and New Haven and Hartford, Connecticut, in an unusual display of unity, declared war on the
Pequots. Each colony contributed armed units. Most of the
units were accompanied by friendly Indians who served as
guides, trackers and interpreters as well as mercenary soldiers.

It was a one-sided, bloody little war. The white colonists
had superiority in arms and in numbers and the Pequots were
systematically eliminated. Pequot leaders were slain, their
villages destroyed, their survivors scattered. The victorious
colonists then seized and occupied the Pequot lands "by right
of conquest." It was a war which demonstrated that the Christian colonists, when put to the test, could be just as ruthless,
just as vengeful, and just as wantonly unforgiving as their
pagan enemies.

An offshoot of the Pequot War was the movement to formalize the collaboration of the several colonies. The movement dawdled for a few years, snagged on petty squabbles. But another Indian scare in 1642 revived interest. There was nothing like the peril of a common enemy to make the colonists forget their petty differences and decide to get together.

So it came to pass that in the spring of 1643 delegates from Plymouth, Massachusetts, and New Haven, Connecticut, met at Boston and formed the New England Confederation.

Rhode Island had joined the others in fighting the Pequot War. The Rhode Island leaders and soldiers were as aggressive and brave as any during that conflict. Nevertheless, Rhode Island supported radical ideas about democracy and freedom of conscience which did not sit well at that time in the other colonies, so Rhode Island was not invited to join the new Confederation. For many years Rhode Island was a pariah colony, scorned and derided by the other colonies, especially by the Puritans in Massachusetts who referred to Rhode Island as "that sewer."

For the next three decades or so relations between the white colonists and the neighboring Indians were fairly amicable. There were flare-ups now and then, occasions when Indians resorted to thievery and the colonists responded with gunfire. And at one point there was a widespread scare when watchers in Connecticut spread the alarm that various Indian tribes were plotting to join forces and attack all of the white settlements in New England. The colonies went on the alert. Massachusetts authorities took the precaution of disarming all the Indians within their jurisdiction. This scare, like so many others, proved groundless.

An uneasy relationship persisted. Despite the fact that a few Indians became close friends of the colonists and learned to speak English, a deep distrust divided most of the Indians and colonists.

Attempts to convert the Indians to Christianity were almost a total failure. The conversion project was even placed on a legal basis with creation in London of The Corporation for Propagating the Gospel in New England. It was financed by a wealthy Englishman, Henry Ashurst, won the blessing of the King, and of course had the eager support of those Puritans who were filled with missionary zeal.

Unfortunately, all of this was so much wasted effort. The trouble was that the Indians were innately immune to Puritan blandishment. They disliked the Puritan ideas of toil, drudgery, and prayer, and they were not persuaded that the white man's religion was superior to their own. As a result, only a handful of Indians adjusted to the new circumstance, put aside their hostility, and collaborated with the newcomers. Even fewer became practicing Christians.

John Winthrop, Jr., governor of Connecticut and son of the Massachusetts governor, developed, and had high hopes for, a program under sponsorship of the Corporation for Propagating the Gospel. His program sought to win over the loyalty of the Indians, first by putting them to useful work in the Puritan communities, then by gradually introducing them to Christianity. But it didn't pan out. Winthrop gave up in despair when he became convinced that the Indians were utterly incapable of sustained labor.

Even more disheartening was the evidence that many of those Indians who professed (namely, accepted) Christianity could not be trusted to have accepted it in good faith. Backsliding seemed to be a common trait.

This situation caused the commissioners of the United Colonies to issue a rueful statement in which they announced:

Wee ever have put a great difference betwixt Indians who professe Jesus Christ and others who declare against Him. But many Indian professers have proved to be loose and falce.

Throughout this period it was abundantly clear that the colonists considered themselves a superior class, God's chosen people. Their egoism knew no limits. William Stoughton expressed the sentiment in a sermon at Boston in 1678 when he boasted that "God sifted a whole nation that he might send choice grain over here into the wilderness." It comforted the colonists to be told they were the "choice grain" selected by divine intercession. Such assurance bolstered their confidence in themselves and their conviction that the native Indians were only savage beasts. In gracious moments the colonists might concede that some Indians might be converted to Christianity. But the converted savages could never hope to escape the blight of their former status, and therefore could never hope to achieve a status of full equality with their superior white tutors.

King Philip's War

A lengthy period of relative calm between colonists and Indians came to an abrupt end in 1675 with the outbreak of King Philip's War.

The Wampanoag tribe of Indians occupied a considerable tract lying roughly between the Plymouth colony and Narragansett Bay. Their chief was a forceful sachem named Metacomet. At some point Metacomet acquired the name "King Philip" and this became his usual designation among the colonists.

King Philip developed a strong dislike for the white colonists. He suspected they had slain his brother, Wamsutta, and he became increasingly annoyed by their apparently insatiable demand for more and more Wampanoag territory.

One Wampanoag Indian became friendly with the white colonists and eventually was converted to Christianity. For a considerable time this Indian served as a spy and informer, tipping off his white friends about doings in the Wampanoag tribe. This arrangement came to a sudden end when the spying activities were disclosed and the tipster was slain by his fellow Wampanoags. In response, the colonists seized three Wampanoags and executed them. That touched off King Philip's War.

King Philip had taken the precaution to line up other Indian tribes as allies. As a result, the war that started in a relatively restricted area occupied by the Wampanoags soon spread to other tribes and eventually encompassed most of New England.

It was a terrifying period for the colonists as the Indians went on the warpath, burning, looting, and killing, even in distant inland settlements. John Pynchon in far-away Springfield reported:

"The hazards are great. If we but stir out for wood, to be shot down by some skulking Indian."

An estimated three thousand five hundred Indians took part in the war. They were vastly outnumbered by the whites. A

61

crude census of 1675, compiled by the Committee of Trade of the Privy Council, put the total white population of the New England region at "about 120 thousand Souls, 16 thousand that can bear Armes." Thus the Indians probably were outnumbered by three-to-one or more. They however, were expert at stealth, setting ambushes, and at camouflage.

Daniel Gookin complained that the Indians did not fight fairly. "Our men could see no enemy to shoot at," he explained, "because the Indians would apparel themselves from the waist upwards with green boughs." This camouflage confused the pursuing colonists, Gookin pointed out, "because they could not readily discern the Indians from the natural bushes." William Hubbard also found the colonists at a disadvantage because the Indians were more familiar with the terrain. "The eyes of the colonists are muffled with the leaves," Hubbard wrote, "and their arms pinioned with the thick boughs of trees, their feet continually shackled with rootes. It is ill fighting with a wild beast in his own den."

Savagery was widespread and the death toll was high on both sides. At last, when the Indians had suffered enormously and were clearly put to rout, King Philip sought to hide out at Bristol, Rhode Island but a treacherous member of his own tribe tipped off the English as to his whereabouts.

King Philip was captured, slain, drawn and quartered – and his head was chopped off the body and displayed atop a pole at Plymouth. That gruesome gesture served both as a proud symbol of the colonists' victory and as a grim warning to any Indians who might get ideas about molesting the colonists in the future.

In the aftermath of King Philip's War, the Puritans examined their situation and concluded that their ordeal was a divine punishment visited upon them because of their own unrepented sins. In short, they figured that if they had just been more pious and less sinful they might not have been forced into the costly war.

The Rev. Increase Mather, pastor of the North Church in Boston and one of the colony's most distinguished prelates, accepted this judgment. Citing the widespread destruction of property and the heavy loss of life, he preached that God had brought on the war as a just punishment for his backsliding people.

The General Court of Massachusetts also endorsed that view. In a resolution adopted in November 1675 the Court admitted that the colony had ignored earlier warnings. "God hath heightened our calamity," the court declared, "and given commission to the barbarous heathen to rise up against us, and to become a smart rod and severe scourge to us."

Many years later, another famous preacher, Cotton Mather, assembled evidence to prove his thesis that a Godly community with a good minister and a strong church was the best security against Indian attack. He pointed out that "those places where the Indian devastation had been most severe were the more pagan skirts of New England where no minister of God was countenanced." He found that settlements with churches "have generally been under more sensible Protection of Heaven," whereas settlements without proper churches often have been "utterly broken up." The lesson was clear: Every settlement must have a good minister and a strong church.

Down through the years it has been customary and convenient to ascribe the worst savagery to the native Indians and to ignore the brutal activities often perpetrated by the white, Christian colonists. This is a lop-sided judgment. The fact is that there was savagery on both sides. In many instances, white men beat, robbed, enslaved, and murdered Indians.

The earlier explorers from Europe sometimes seized and bound Indians like wild animals, carrying them off to Europe as trophies. (Squanto, the Indian at Plymouth, apparently had been one of these earlier captives who later, by some means, was returned to America.)

During the Pequot War, colonial militiamen attacked an Indian village in southern Connecticut, killed the adult Pequot males, destroyed the Indian village, then shipped off the Pequot women and children to be sold as slaves in the West Indies.

Atrocities on both sides also were frequent during King Philip's War - including the spiteful and repugnant treatment meted out by the colonists on their defeated foe, King Philip.

Who Owns the Land?

Over a span of centuries, explorers who discovered uncharted lands claimed those lands for God and monarch. It was the standard practice. Since God was not present in person to exercise His share of the claim, the practical result was that the monarch - whether King or Queen - became the undisputed proprietor of the new lands and could do with them whatever seemed appropriate.

The usual pattern then was for the monarch to award grants or patents to friends, relatives, or properly obsequious companies of adventurers. In this way, vast hunks of America were handed out. Now nobody at the time knew much about the size of America. There were no reliable maps and the geographical points of reference often were muddled. As a result, the various royal grants frequently overlapped and the boundaries were in dispute.

When the Puritans came over in 1630, their royal charter at Massachusetts Bay gave them authority over a swath that extended westward, presumably to the Pacific Ocean. Puritan leaders under the charter were empowered to allocate land in this domain as they saw fit, and this they proceeded to do.

But what about the native Indians? Wasn't the land theirs? Well, the colonists recognized in a sort of loose and flexible way that the resident Indians, if any, might have some prior right of ownership of the land. So, in an effort to make the deal orderly, attempts usually were made to find the resident Indians and buy the land from them. All of the settlements around Massachusetts Bay, as well as the earliest settlements on the Connecticut River and in Rhode Island, were on land purchased in this fashion from resident Indians. (Let's not quibble about land prices. In the 1600's an iron skillet and a couple of hand mirrors might be worth several hundred acres of land.)

Not all the land taken over by the colonists was acquired by purchase. There were instances – as at Plymouth – where the colonists could not locate any local tribe that might own the land. There were other places where the colonists simply moved in as squatters and took over without bothering to inquire about previous owners.

Puritan leaders rationalized these informal procedures. Francis Higginson noted that the Indians did a great deal of moving about and couldn't possibly own all the land they used only occasionally. John Cotton took this thesis a step forward. Anyone "who taketh possession of vacant land and bestoweth culture and husbandry upon it" has an inviolable right to that land, Mr. Cotton declared.

John Winthrop agreed. He argued that the Indians were entitled only to as much land as they could occupy and improve. "The rest of the country," he insisted, "lies open to any who could and would improve it."

Clearly the white colonists who were bringing "culture and husbandry" to a backward land felt that their rights were paramount. They were quite willing to observe the niceties of buying the land they wanted if it was convenient to do so. But if formal purchase was not convenient, the colonists didn't hesitate to exercise their superior rights. They simply moved in and took over.

Finally, there were the parcels of land seized "by right of conquest." A basic tenet among Europeans at the time – a tenet accepted by the colonists – was that the winner in a war had the right to seize the property of the loser. This was considered a God-given right. We find it exercised in June 1637, immediately after the Pequot War, when the Connecticut General Court ordered thirty men to the territory formerly occupied by the Pequots. The action was taken, the Court explained, "to maynteine our right that God by conquest hath given us." Included in this land grab was the present site of New London, Connecticut, and a strip of shoreline extending perhaps forty miles (there were no precise measurements) to the westward.

The matter of land purchase took a curious turn at Windsor, Connecticut. Puritan settlers from Dorchester, near Boston, went west to the valley of the Connecticut in 1635 and purchased several square miles of land from a Paquanick sachem named Sehat. On this tract they founded the town of Windsor, just north of Hartford on the Connecticut River. The land purchase deal apparently was satisfactory at the time both to the colonists and to the Paquanicks.

Thirty years later, however, in a deed dated March 31, 1665, a leader of the Windsor colony, William Phelps, explained: "I now engage to make up the full payment by paying to the said Sehat's kinsman, Nassahegan, sachem of the Paquanicks, four trucking coats, or whatever upon agreement shall satisfy them to the value thereof." In return, Nassahegan was to guarantee the land free of challenge from him, his successors, his heirs "or any other Indian or Indians whatsoever."

Maybe the Indians felt they had been cheated in the

original 1635 deal and demanded more. Or maybe the colonists, after thirty years, were troubled by their own consciences and decided to sweeten the original purchase price.

* * * * *

Any examination of these land deals in the Sixteenth Century runs smack dab into a local curiosity. It is, simply, that the American Indians did not have the foggiest notion what the colonists meant by land purchase. To the Indians, the land was a fixture in their firmament like the air above or the waters of the sea. One didn't own or trade the land any more than one owned or traded the air.

Yet, here came these white men with the strange idea that land could be bought, sold, traded and owned like a basket of beans. There is reason to believe that in the original land deals the Indians didn't understand at all that they were selling a piece of land. They didn't even know they owned the land to begin with. They probably thought the colonists were offering gifts (a common Indian practice) for the right to be left unmolested (also a custom the Indians understood.)

Much later, as the Indians became more sophisticated, they caught on to the white man's idea about land ownership, but in the first encounters it was to them just a puzzling practice they couldn't grasp.

Pesky Neighbors

Indians were not the only troublesome people encountered by the English colonists in New England. A wary eye also had to be kept on other Europeans who had been attracted to America.

The Spaniards and the Portuguese were no problem. Their interest in the New World lay far to the south and they paid little attention to New England. But Dutchmen and Frenchmen pressed uncomfortably close to the English settlements. Just to the south, the Dutch settled at the mouth of the Hudson River and were making moves to expand. Just to the north, the French established their New France in what is now Canada; they, too, had expansionist plans. Thus the English colonists in New England found themselves uneasily fronted by Dutch to the south and by French to the north. And relations with these neighbors were not necessarily harmonious.

This was a period of great instability in international affairs. That's the diplomatic way of observing that the various nations of Europe were at each other's throats much of the time.

At any given moment, England, France, Portugal, Holland, and Spain might be at war. Any pair might be going at it, or any grouping of two or three might be ganging up on a fourth. It was like a game of dice. No one knew from one month to the next what combinations of enemies and allies, foes and friends, might turn up.

Wars were declared, perhaps with ample justification but often because of some fancied insult or because of a monarch's whim. Peace was proclaimed if one side was clearly the victor. In other circumstances, though, peace might come to pass if a satisfactory quantity of gold accompanied an apology. Or maybe peace would result if a suitable princess was found to wed a suitable prince and thus bind the belligerent nations in a nuptial bond.

Nations which were officially at peace generally were expected to refrain from hostile activity and to respect each other's property. But that amicable situation was seldom obtained. Frequently, the strong were tempted to attack and plunder the weak whether the two parties happened to be at peace or not.

On the high seas especially the rules of peace, if there were any, were blithely ignored. Rapacious sea dogs sailing armed vessels roamed the waterways of the world capturing anything they could catch. They were pirates and brigands whose game was to plunder, and when they returned to their homelands with their loot they were hailed as heroes.

Francis Drake was one of the most successful pirates. His specialty was capturing Spanish ships laden with gold and silver from Mexico and the West Indies. In 1577 he set forth on a raiding expedition with five vessels. Four of the ships dropped out. But Drake kept on in the fifth vessel – the *Golden Hind*. He managed to round Cape Horn, ravish a few Spanish settlements on the west coast of South America, sail on across the Pacific to the Orient, and eventually – after an absence of three years – return to England with his vessel bulging with loot.

Queen Elizabeth was delighted. Her eyes sparkled when she examined the plunder estimated to be worth more than one million pounds, a splendid haul. The Queen was pleased to give a cut to Drake, then stash the rest away in the royal stores. In addition, the Queen expressed her gratitude by knighting the pirate hero – making him Sir Francis Drake. (The Queen's love life always has been something of a mystery. There is some reason to suspect she may have had something more than just a formal, business-like relationship with the famous brigand.)

No one ever questioned Drake's courage. He demonstrated it again a few years later when he was involved in an exciting exploit:

Word leaked out that Spain had reached the end of its patience. It was fed up with all the indignities imposed by pirates who regularly held up Spanish ships and stole the treasures the Spaniards had just stolen in America. Equally irritating was the refusal of Queen Elizabeth even to answer their formal complaints. So Spain decided to build a fleet of warships, attack England and properly punish that nest of thieves. When the English got wind of this scheme, they lined up a fleet of thirty vessels and put Drake in command. Sir Francis sailed this fleet boldly into the harbor of Cadiz in 1587, shot up the place, and destroyed the vessels the Spaniards were building there. Back at home in England, Drake was lionized for his bold success and applauded lustily when he boasted how he had "singed the beard of the Spanish King."

Spain was deeply humiliated and the King, Philip II, was furious. He pressed for retaliation, ordering that a huge fleet of one hundred and thirty vessels be built. This was the great Spanish Armada which sailed for England in 1588 but was routed by British defenders off the English coast in one of the most famous sea battles in history. Sir Francis Drake directed the victorious English fleet.

An Uneasy Colony

For the colonists in New England, all this activity in far-away Europe and in distant seas might seem to be about as significant as happenings on another planet. Indeed, communication was so slow that news of war or peace or anything else took six to ten weeks to cross from England to the colonies. The colonists thus were insulated by both time and distance from happenings in their homeland.

Nevertheless, the colonists were affected because many of those events in the Old World had an echo effect in the New. The colonists were aware, for example, that if France and England were at war - not an uncommon situation - the French in Canada might get ideas about attacking the English settlements in Massachusetts. It worked the other way, too. The colonists in New England still considered themselves loyal subjects of the English monarch, even if they did not like him much, and if they learned that England and France were at war, they would feel an obligation to attack the French enemies in America as best they could.

Early in 1633, when the English at Massachusetts Bay had been settled less than three years, they heard disturbing rumors that the French up north were planning an attack. In response, the Massachusetts General Court decided to erect a fortified town at Natascott "to be some block in an enemy's way," and to authorize a new settlement at Agawam "lest an enemy, finding it void, should possess and take it from us."

It so happened that nothing developed from this particular scare. But the colonists felt that the potential peril was real, not imaginary, and in the decades that followed the English colonists had ample reason to be suspicious of those French adventurers on their northern doorstep. Periods of tension and hostility between them were more frequent than periods of amity. Over a span of more than one hundred years, brushes between the French and English were common, and on many occasions they developed into full-scale battles.

French Incursions

The French were by no means Johnnies-come-lately on the American scene. In fact, they were busily exploring, fishing and fur-trading in their New France long before the Puritans settled Massachusetts in their New England.

As early as 1603 a remarkable Frenchman known as Sieur de Monts, who was a wealthy friend of King Henry IV, obtained a royal monopoly on American trade and began exploring the New World for France. He made several voyages to America, became familiar with the northern reaches and explored down the coast as far as Cape Cod.

Another remarkable Frenchman, Samuel de Champlain, began as a disciple of Sieur de Monts but soon surpassed his mentor in fame and achievement. Beginning in 1603, Champlain made many voyages to America. He explored the coast of New England, drew charts of the Maine coast, directed a fur-trading enterprise, travelled up the St. Lawrence River and made friends with the Huron Indians. In 1608 he placed French settlers at the site of Quebec, thus establishing the first permanent French settlement in America.

In 1611 Champlain set up an Indian trading post at the present site of Montreal. Two years later – always an explorer with itchy feet – he tramped much deeper into the New World to study the broad and attractive area around the Great Lakes.

English adventurers, on the prowl in northern America during one of the frequent periods of English-French hostility, attacked and captured Quebec in 1629. Champlain was seized and carried back to England where he was held as a prisoner-exile for three years. When France and England settled their differences and signed a peace treaty in 1632, New France was restored and Champlain was returned to America. He died in 1635 and was buried in Quebec, an honorable man described as "the father of New France."

Other French explorers followed Champlain's lead. Jean de Brebeuf, a Jesuit missionary, journeyed to Quebec in 1625 and became closely associated with the Huron Indians as friend and teacher. Jacques Marquette, also a Jesuit missionary, sailed to New France in 1666, explored a huge stretch of territory, and discovered the upper reaches of the Mississippi River. His findings opened the way for Rene Robert Cavelier La Salle who, in 1682, sailed down the length of the Mississippi River. At the site of present-day New Orleans, La Salle set his pennant and claimed the entire Mississippi Valley for God and the King of France. La Salle named the area Louisiana.

At this moment in history the French had nailed down an excellent claim to become the dominant power in North America. Their control and influence covered enormous tracts: Canada, the Great Lakes area, the Mississippi Valley, and Louisiana. But the French had a critical weakness: while they were superb at exploring, trading, and winning the confidence of the native Indians, they were less successful at colonizing. Their settlements usually were weak and insecure. In the end it was the English who proved to be the more successful colonists, and colonization proved to be the key to dominance on the continent.

The Dutch Foothold

Dutchmen from the Netherlands, like the French, had a foothold in North America long before the Puritans reached Massachusetts. Henry Hudson in 1609 and Adriaen Block in 1610 established claims for Holland and set up trading posts on the Hudson River.

(It is one of the strange twists of history that Holland's early claims to land in America rested largely on the explorations of Henry Hudson, an Englishman, and that England's early claims rested largely on the explorations of John Cabot, an Italian. Navigators and explorers back in those days weren't picky, they were quite willing to hire out to any employer-monarch so long as the rewards were satisfactory. That is why Hudson, the Englishman, worked for Holland, while Cabot, the Italian, worked for England.)

Long before it cast its eyes in the direction of America, Holland had established a fine record in the business of grabbing control of distant lands. Holland set up its Dutch East India Company in 1602. It did this to protect its trading posts and other holdings in Java and Malaysia from marauding English, Spanish, and Portuguese operators. The Dutch East India Company was enormously successful. It not only beat off the marauders but managed to extend its influence into Japan, China, India, and Persia.

Emboldened by this success in the Far East, and encouraged by the prospects its traders saw in America, Holland, in 1621, chartered its Dutch West India Company. It hoped its West company would match the success of its company in the East.

Under the guidance of the Dutch West India Company, fortified trading posts were established at Fort Orange (now Albany) and at other points on the Hudson River. All of these holdings were incorporated as New Netherlands.

Peter Minuit was sent over in 1626 to be governor of this new Dutch colony. He never achieved greatness as an administrator or as anything else, but he did win a unique place in history as the fellow who bought Manhattan Island from the Canarsee Indians for twenty-four dollars' worth of trinkets. Debates have raged ever since over who got the best of the deal, though both sides at the time considered it a fair transaction. Anyhow, time has proved that Minuit guessed right when he selected lower Manhattan as the site of his settlement to be called New Amsterdam. Of course it was only a collection of rude shacks in his time. But it grew. How it grew!

Meanwhile, back in Holland efforts were made to encourage families to migrate to New Netherlands. The government offered huge tracts of land in America to any "patroon" who could get fifty families to sign up as settlers. The idea was to create a sort of modified feudal system. The patroon was to be lord of the manor, and the families laboring for him would have a status something like indentured servants. A considerable number of Hollanders came over under this arrangement. But the patroon system was not well-suited to the New World and it soon withered away and passed from the scene.

Relations between the English and Dutch colonists were quite friendly much of the time. One of Peter Minuit's first projects at New Amsterdam in 1626 was to set up a mutually agreeable trading arrangement with the English settlers up the coast at Plymouth.

In subsequent years, New Amsterdam developed into a busy, polyglot trading center. Vessels from many parts of the world stopped in bearing exotic wares. One visitor reported hearing eighteen different languages spoken on the street. The English at Conneticut, Rhode Island, and Massachusetts regularly traversed the Sound in their sailing craft to trade at New Amsterdam where goods were available in great variety.

Nevertheless, the English colonists were never quite comfortable with the situation. No matter how neighborly the Dutch might be, they were still regarded as aliens. What's more, the English felt that their own claims in America were much superior to the Dutch claims. In English eyes, all of those Dutchmen at New Amsterdam and on the upper Hudson were interlopers squatting on English soil. For much of this period, however, England was warring with France or with Spain and it did not want to add to its problems by antagonizing the Dutch at New Amsterdam. So the English held their peace. Restraint was exercised even on several testy occasions when English and Dutch parties became embroiled in spats on the Sound, across the way on Long Island, and along the Connecticut River.

Finally, in 1650, delegations from the two sides met at Hartford and agreed on a treaty. A line was drawn on the map from the west side of Greenwich harbor stretching northward into the interior and southward across Long Island. Lands to the west of the line were to be Dutch; lands to the east were to be English. The boundary treaty was signed Sept. 19, 1650. (It probably was the first international boundary in American history.)

The agreement required ratification by the governments in England and in the Netherlands. The Netherlands government did ratify the treaty later on, but it may be significant that the English government never did.

Another throw of the dice changed the picture in July 1652 when England declared war on the Netherlands. (The issue was a complicated one of maritime rights.)

The colonies in America this time were left to decide for themselves whether they would engage in this war or not. Both New Amsterdam and Boston preferred not. Both valued their friendly trading, both shied from the prospect of warfare, and neither could work up any enthusiasm for this latest quarrel in Europe.

The sentiment was far different, however, in those English settlements close to the Dutch domain. Here the war scare was real. New Haven was terrified by the prospect that the Dutch might turn loose their Indian allies to ravage the countryside. In a tearful plea for help, New Haven called upon Massachusetts for support, but the plea stirred no sympathy in Boston.

Events took a more serious turn in June 1654 when two armed English vessels sailed into Boston harbor bearing an impressive assortment of official proclamations. The ships were authorized to attack the Dutch at New Amsterdam. But before the attack could be launched, word reached Boston that England and the Netherlands had signed a peace treaty. The war was over. And the two armed English vessels at Boston sailed back to England without having fired a shot.

The English colonists still found the Dutch domain so close to them a pesky nuisance. Moreover, the English stoutly maintained that the Dutch were interlopers on territory that was properly English.

A direct challenge to Dutch claims was made in 1659 by the Massachusetts General Court. The genesis of the challenge apparently was the desire of some Puritans to press their influence westward to the Hudson River. In any case, the Massachusetts Court drew up and approved a blunt message to Peter Stuyvesant at New Amsterdam. The message argued that many parts of the Hudson valley claimed by the Dutch were not "actually possessed." It further declared: "Wee conceive that no reason can be imagined why we should not improve and make use of our just rightes in all of the landes granted us."

The belligerency of this note may be misleading. It is quite true that the English government was hostile toward the Dutch, but the English colonists in America generally did not share this hostility at all. It seems likely, therefore, that the government in London ordered or nudged the Court at Boston to deliver that sharp note to New Amsterdam.

New York Established

Be that as it may, King Charles II settled the problem of New Amsterdam once and for all. In 1664 he gave his brother, the Duke of York, all the territory occupied by the Dutch in America and he ordered the Duke to take it over. Just like that.

The Duke demurred. "We are not at war with them," he pointed out.

But the King was firm. "It has never been their land," he declared. "It is ours. They are living on our land."

The Duke of York had no taste for war or for long ocean voyages. The comforts of palace life were much more agreeable to him. So the Duke stayed at home when he dispatched his fleet of warships to seize New Netherlands as the King had ordered.

On September 4, 1664, the Duke's English fleet sailed into the harbor at New Amsterdam. This was a war of conquest involving two of the great powers of Europe. But it also was a comic opera episode in American history in which the grins far outnumbered the frowns.

The plain fact is that neither side was itching for a fight. Both thought the prospect of a party at the shorefront ale houses was more attractive than any set-to with shot, shell, or fisticuffs. So after a good deal of sputtering ashore, while the English ships of war paraded in the harbor like fighting roosters, the Dutch were persuaded that they were outmanned and outgunned and that resistance would be futile. Besides, the English offered attractive terms: no seizure of property, no jailing of dissidents, full liberty of conscience for all inhabitants.

Thus New Netherlands surrendered its domain in North America. It went out not with a bang but with a sigh. The name of the territory was changed to New York and the English flag was raised.

Peter Stuyvesant had a farm in Manhattan. He retired from politics after his surrender and lived out the rest of his life on his rural acres in the New York that had once been his New Netherlands.

One other aspect of this event deserves mention. John Winthrop, Jr., governor of Connecticut and son of the leader at Boston, had a prominent part in negotiating the transfer of authority from the Dutch to the English under York. The junior Winthrop was a Puritan. He had supported his father in all of the early work of setting up the colony in Massachusetts. But the younger Winthrop was not nearly as autocratic, as dogmatic, and as stubbornly pious as his father. He was a moderate man with an open mind. In several of the quarrels that beset the struggling colonies the younger Winthrop emerged as the conciliator who pointed to the just solution and did it in a way that won the respect of both sides.

There is room to believe that the younger Winthrop applied his skills as a conciliator between the Dutch and the English. We know from the record that he was in contact with both sides. And we can surmise that it was he who persuaded his Dutch friends on the futilty of resisting the English incursion, and that it also was he who persuaded the English attackers to offer generous terms.

It is especially significant that those peace terms included full liberty of conscience for all the citizens in the Dutch territory now being taken over by the English. Such liberty of conscience was still anathema in Puritan Boston, still scorned as an evil by most of the Puritan preachers. But the younger John Winthrop accepted it, endorsed it, and promoted it. Unlike his father, who was set in his ways, the younger Winthrop saw values in moderation and toleration which were beginning to take root in New England.

* * * * *

Indian support was an important factor in all the pulling, hauling, and quarrelling among Dutch, French, and English in colonial America. Each explorer, each wandering trader, and each batch of settlers usually managed to establish friendly relations with some of the Indians. In the skirmishes that broke out from time to time, Indian allies usually accompanied the white colonial skirmishers. On some occasions, Indian mercenaries did all the skirmishing under white direction.

The French were most skillful in winning support of the Indians. At no time after 1630 did the French have nearly so many of their countrymen in America as did the English and the Dutch. But the French compensated for this lack in numbers by enlisting considerable groups of Indians to their cause and thus usually were able to hold their own in the bickering over boundaries or whatever.

In the end, both the Dutch and the French lost influence and lost territory. Only some parts of Canada and a few place names – such as Des Plaines, Cape Girardeau, Baton Rouge, and Louisiana – are reminders of the period when Frenchmen dominated much of the New World.

Similarly, only a few place names – such as Brooklyn, Yonkers, and Tappan Zee – are reminders of the New Netherlands colony in the Seventeenth Century.

CHAPTER FOUR

BIOGRAPHICAL SKETCHES

Three colonists deserve special attention for their influence on early New England: Roger Williams, Anne Hutchinson, and Samuel Gorton. All three settled first in the Bay colony. All three uttered unpopular views. All three were banished. But their arguments, their disputes, and their banishment had a far-reaching impact which hastened the trend toward tolerance in New England.

Roger Williams

Roger Williams, a young scholar trained in the ministry, sailed from England in early December of 1630 and reached Nantasket, near Boston, eight weeks later. His credentials were satisfactory and he was hired as a teacher in the church at Salem.

Williams was a brash and testy individual. He was blessed with an enormous ego and an abundance of self confidence. Right at the start he caused quite a stir when he rejected that first appointment at Salem on the ground that the congregation there was not sufficiently Puritan. Too many of the practices in that Salem Church, said he, echoed practices of the despised Church of England. The distinguished elders of the Salem church were astonished and not a little annoyed by this brazen display.

So Williams quit Salem in a huff and marched down the coast to the settlement at Plymouth. He found this colony slightly more congenial. After preaching there for a year, however, he managed to wear out his welcome. Elders at the Plymouth church became disenchanted with his "strange opinions" and made it clear that they would just as soon see him depart.

In 1633 Williams - apparently forgiven for his earlier rudeness - was called back to Salem to assist in the ministry. It wasn't long, though, before he was in hot water again. First, he raised a ruckus by charging that the original charter for the Massachusetts Bay colony was invalid. It was invalid, he declared, because the King had no authority to make such grants of land. The land in America, Williams argued, could be acquired properly only by agreement with the native Americans, the Indians.

There's a nit-picking distinction here. Except in a few cases where settlers appropriated (that is, stole) land in America, the principal colonists did, in fact, parley with the Indians and make payments to buy the land for their colonies. But they did this, of course, only after they had obtained a charter from the King to proceed. The Williams argument was that the original charter was invalid (because the King lacked authority) therefore all the deals that followed also were invalid.

The unorthodox Williams view didn't sit well with the authorities. At least a few of them reached apoplectic levels of indignation. But much more was to follow. There was a strong dose of firebrand in Roger Williams' makeup and he wasn't at all shy about displaying it.

And so it was that, shortly thereafter, Williams startled his congregation by charging that King Charles was an ally of anti-Christ. Most of the colonists at this time had little love for the King, and they heartily despised the Church of England which he supported. Nevertheless, the colonists still considered themselves suhjects of the King. They were hesitant to express any criticism of the crown and they were uncomfortable when they heard anyone else making such criticism. The upshot of this episode was that Williams was called before the General Court and made to apologize for his charge.

Nor was that the end of it. Roger Williams continued to say what he thought, and his thoughts often were in conflict with prevailing opinion.

On October 9, 1635, he was called before the General Court again, this time charged with voicing "new and dangerous opinions against the authority of the magistrates." These "new and dangerous opinions" included the Williams view that church and state should be separate, and the equally unpopular view that every man should be permitted to worship in whatever way he preferred.

That was the last straw. The members of the Court

decided they had suffered enough of this Williams blasphemy so they banished him from the colony. The General Court planned to ship Williams back to England, there being no place in the New World for such a troublemaker. But the culprit slipped away, passed the winter of 1635–36 living with the Indians, and in the spring of 1636 bought some land from the Narragansetts and founded a settlement on Narragansett Bay which was to become Rhode Island.

At the start, Roger Williams was accompanied by only a few close friends and his plans were modest. He thought he might set up a trading post where he could eke out a living by trading with the Indians. The notion of establishing an entirely new colony didn't enter his mind.

But Williams' ideas about democracy and religious freedom attracted followers. Many of them were individuals who had chafed under the rigid rules of Puritan Massachusetts Bay, and quite a few, like Williams, had suffered banishment. Thus it was that the simple Williams trading post expanded rapidly into a settlement as the newcomers trekked in. Soon it began to take on the look of a colony with communities at Providence and at Newport – the extremities of Narragansett Bay – and other smaller settlements appearing up and down the shores of the bay.

For several years the Roger Williams domain rocked along in only a loosely-organized fashion. The situation might better be described as a loosely-disorganized fashion because there was no central government and no code of laws applying to the entire area. Then in 1643 Williams recognized that what had developed here was a colony and that it surely needed a more substantial base. So he sailed off to England, sought out some influential friends and they persuaded the King to give Williams a royal charter.

That was the beginning of Rhode Island as a legitimate chartered colony. And it was a remarkable colony indeed. W. E. Woodward, the historian, has described it in these words:

> *It was the only place in the civilized world where a citizen could comport himself as one does in the United States today. No one had to go to church, everyone could vote, a man could enter any trade or calling. There was no censorship of papers or books.*

The Jews who were unwelcome in other communities found a haven in Rhode Island, and the first synagogue in the New World was built at Newport.

The Quakers, who had been hounded, terrorized and persecuted in Massachusetts, also found a peaceful atmosphere in Rhode Island. They built a meeting house on Jamestown Island, below Providence, which, three hundred years later, was restored as an important historic relic of the colonial period.

Roger Williams continued to operate his trading post and to pursue his studies of Indian lore. He learned the language of the Narragansetts and wrote an Indian dictionary. But his lasting contribution was in establishing the first truly tolerant community in the New World. This was a community that separated church and state, that placed no rules on the manner in which a person worshipped, and that offered fellowship to newcomers of any religious faith.

The stricter Puritan communities around Boston and in Connecticut looked upon Rhode Island with contempt. They often referred to it as "Rogue's Island" or described it as "that sewer". But the tolerance which found a footing in Rhode Island outlasted the intolerance that dominated the older settlements. Ultimately the Rhode Island way prevailed in the next century when the Founding Fathers set about erecting a new nation.

Anne Hutchinson

History counts quite a few vigorously energetic women who flashed upon the scene with wildly controversial opinions, won many fanatical followers and stirred up violent opposition before passing from the scene. One thinks of Joan of Arc, Mary Baker Eddy, Carrie Nation, and Aimee Semple McPherson.

Anne Hutchinson, a Seventeenth Century matron, belongs in that group. She was the wife of William Hutchinson, a successful merchant, and, for much of her life, she lived quietly as a housewife in Lincolnshire, England.

In middle age, Mrs. Hutchinson became deeply absorbed in religion. She ceased to be just a quiet housewife and became, instead, an enthusiastic and indefatigable agitator for the Puritan faith. Mrs. Hutchinson was thoroughly versed in Puritan theology. She knew the Bible backward and forward, loved to debate points of scripture, and particularly enjoyed every chance to out-wit, out-argue, and out-shout any male foolish enough to challenge her.

The Rev. John Cotton was pastor of the little Lincolnshire church which the Hutchinsons attended. And he was the lady's mentor. Mrs. Hutchinson hung on every word Mr. Cotton uttered, listened with rapt attention to his sermons, and memorized many of them.

There came a day when Mr. Cotton packed his bags, bid his congregation farewell and sailed off to America. Mrs. Hutchinson took the departure badly. A new minister appeared at her church, and while she found his doctrine acceptable, she felt that he lacked the fire, conviction and appeal of Mr. Cotton.

So one night when her husband William came home from work, she informed him that she was starved for spiritual satisfaction and that they must journey to America to re-join Mr. Cotton's flock in the New World. That was it. Her mind was made up.

William did not put much stock in religious fervor. It seemed to him that one pastor's sermons were pretty much like all the others, and he never did quite understand why his wife got so worked up about scriptural nit-picking. But he was an easy-going man and he wanted peace in the family. So in a matter of weeks he managed to sell out his mercantile interests, dispose of his property and book passage to America. He and his wife sailed across the Atlantic in 1635.

In Boston, the Hutchinsons rejoined Mr. Cotton and became parishioners in his church. Almost immediately, however, Mrs. Hutchinson stirred up a hornets' nest of trouble. She organized a sort of women's club, conducted regular meetings at her home and expounded her religious ideas. The women of Boston were thrilled by this diversion. They became her enthusiastic supporters.

The trouble was that Anne was teaching what was called the Covenant of Grace. This didn't square with the Covenant of Works, which was the accepted doctrine in Puritan theology. Now these points of theology can become terribly confusing as they veer off into abstractions and mysticisms. Let us attempt to simplify a complex matter with brief descriptions. The Covenant of Works held that a person would be judged, both in this world and in the hereafter, by his deeds, or works. Anne Hutchinson's Covenant of Grace, on the other hand, insisted that works didn't matter. Instead, she argued that no matter what a person did in this life, no matter how good and important his "works," that person was not a pure Christian unless he had an inner life that was full of grace. It was never quite clear how one obtained this grace. Nor was it ever quite clear how a person's grace could be measured - to determine whether he or she was or wasn't full of it.

This is the sort of philosophical puzzle the colonists enjoyed in the Seventeenth Century. They devoted hours and hours to this tossing of complicated ideas back and forth with a fanatic such as Mrs. Hutchinson on one side and the entrenched Puritan bigots on the other, the stage was prepared for a first-class brouhaha. It didn't take long for the situation to become intolerable with the fur flying and the air filled with bitter invective.

Governor Winthrop made his position perfectly clear. He told the General Court that Anne Hutchinson was "an instrument of Satan fitted and trained for her service to poison the churches here planted." Obviously, in his view, there could be no place in the colony for such a blatant heretic.

The upshot was that Mrs. Hutchinson was brought to trial in November 1637, convicted of heresy and banished from the colony.

Perhaps the experience drained away all of her missionary passion. In any case, she and her husband moved to Rhode Island. Her husband continued as a successful merchant, and Anne settled back into the quiet life of a housewife, never again one to challenge the church or lead a religious crusade.

After her husband's death, she moved to New York and settled in a house in what is now Westchester. The Indians in the neiggborhood appeared friendly and Anne frequently gave them gifts of food or clothing. But one day the Indians went on a rampage, attacked her house and killed her and all the others in her household.

When the Boston Puritans heard this news, they assured one another with smug satisfaction that the slaying was surely a proper judgment of God.

Samuel Gorton

The differences that Roger Williams and Anne Hutchinson had with the Puritan leaders were trivial differences compared to the disagreements stirred up by Samuel Gorton. Here was a man who dared to question the basic premises of Puritan thought. He not only questioned those premises but did so loudly and belligerently.

Samuel Gorton came over to the American colonies from England in 1637 and settled in Boston. He did not last long. His radical views soon made him a pariah in the community and he was booted out.

There was nothing subtle about this clash of opinion. It was as plain as a wart on the nose. Samuel Gorton was a free thinker. He denied the Trinity of Father, Son and Holy Spirit. He insisted that it was purest nonsense to believe that there was an actual heaven or hell. Moreover, Gorton declared that

82

there was no valid role for any priest or minister because every man should communicate directly with God. (This was similar to the Quaker belief.)

Naturally the Puritans were shocked by Gorton's utterances. It was abundantly clear to them that this was a wicked man speaking with the voice of Satan.

After being evicted from Boston, Gorton went south to the Plymouth colony. Many before him had found a haven in Plymouth after banishment in Massachusetts Bay. But Gorton continued to argue his unorthodox views so eloquently and so abrasively that the relatively easy-going leaders at Plymouth also found him unacceptable. They banished him, too. Even Rhode Island, a liberal spot in a sea of sanctimony, looked upon Gorton with some suspicion when he reached there. At one point in 1643 he was captured by a band of soldiers or vigilantes and held briefly as a prisoner.

Ultimately Gorton's case reached England where unidentified supporters persuaded the Earl of Warwick to intervene. The Earl managed to have a royal order promulgated. It ordered the colonies to stop molesting Samuel Gorton.

Gorton then settled on the west shore of Narragansett Bay and established a community. Out of respect for the man in England who had befriended him, he named his community Warwick. It became a part of Rhode Island and still is.

* * * * *

In one way or another, openly or subtly, these three dissidents Roger Williams, Anne Hutchinson and Samuel Gorton - contributed something to progress in America By challenging the orthodox beliefs of the time, they forced the Puritans to consider change and gradually accept change. It was part of the swelling tide that finally swept away the most glaring aspects of intolerance in America.

Others of Note

Many other personalities appeared on the stage in early New England, played out their roles in the infant colony and left their mark on history. Let us consider a few of them here.

John Eliot

As a young man of twenty-seven, John Eliot crossed to

America in 1631 and accepted a post as "teacher" at the church in Roxbury. (Teacher was a word often used by the colonists where we would use pastor, minister or parson.) Mr. Eliot had studied at Cambridge University, had fine credentials and was well-liked by his congregation. What set him apart, though, was his deeply sincere interest in the native Indians. Now of course there were many Puritans who came over with a Godly fire in their eyes and with loud intentions about converting the Indians to Christianity. The difference was that Mr. Eliot was one of the few who persisted in his intention. He refused to quit the cause when the going got tough, as most of the others did.

From his base at Roxbury, Mr. Eliot studied and mastered the language of Indians in that Massachusetts area. He was the first white man to preach to the Indians in the Indian tongue. That was only the start. Mr. Eliot translated the Bible into Indian, persuaded many Indians to convert to Christianity, and with the help of several other ministers established several villages peopled entirely by Christianized Indians.

During the Pequot War, Mr. Eliot's Christianized Indians were in an awkwardly dangerous position. They were despised both by other Indians who considered them traitors and by many colonists who could not accept the conversion as genuine.

Mr. Eliot struggled on, doing his best to protect his flock from the hostility on both sides. He lived out a long and fruitful life and died in 1690 at the age of eighty-six.

Uncas

This Indian chief, sachem of the Mohegan Indians, may have been the smartest, and certainly was the slipperiest, of all the Indians encountered by the colonists in New England. Uncas was sly, devious and vengeful. His word meant nothing. Not for a moment could he be trusted. After a few experiences most of the colonists had him sized up and were on guard for his tricks, but he still managed to out-smart them time after time.

Uncas grew up as a Pequot. About the time that Europeans began to settle in New England, Uncas had a dispute with Sassacus, the Pequot chieftain to whom he was related. Uncas thereupon quit the Pequot tribe, marched away with a few followers and formed the Mohegan tribe. His Mohegan headquarters were along the river not far from the present site of New London, Connecticut.

When the Pequot War broke out in 1637, with the Pequots and the white colonists engaged in bitter combat, Uncas turned his back on the Pequots and sided with the colonists. At the end of the war when the Pequot leaders were slain and their villages ravished, Uncas moved in and claimed his spoils. The few surviving members of the Pequot tribe then joined the Mohegans.

Meanwhile, Uncas had carried on a long and bitter feud with the Narragansett Indians who occupied land to the east of his domain. His particular target was Miantonomo, sachem of the Narragansetts. Both Uncas and Miantonomo had supported the white settlers during the Pequot War and it was to the advantage of the settlers that this feud be laid to rest. So mediation was arranged and was carried out successfully. The two Indian chieftains met under white auspices and agreed to a peace pact.

But Uncas soon violated the terms of the peace pact and renewed the feud. in an especially bold move in 1643, Uncas captured Miantonomo, tied him up as a prisoner, then turned him over to the white colonists at Hartford together with a list of trumped up charges intended to persuade the colonists that Miantonomo had been deceitful and traitorous. The English smelled something fishy in this deal. They promptly freed Miantonomo, then, in a thoughtless move, handed him back to Uncas.

Shortly thereafter, Miantonomo was murdered. This touched off an explosion of controversy. The Narragansetts threatened war on the Pequots to avenge the murder of their chief. There were even rumors that the Narragansetts were so distraught they were preparing to attack white settlements, too. A hasty meeting of the United Colonies was called at Boston and the delegates agreed to put three hundred armed men in the field at once to block the threatening hostilities.

Cooler heads finally prevailed. The Mohegans and the Narragansetts were persuaded, once more, to enter into a peace agreement.

Uncas continued as the leader of his tribe, and continued his harsh, ruthless and deceitful practices. He lived to the age of ninety. By that time his Mohegan tribe had shrunk almost to the point of extinction. It just faded away, as did he.

Two hundred years later the James Fenimore Cooper novels mentioned Uncas and the Mohegans in glowing terms. That was pure fiction. The heroic Uncas of the novels bore little resemblance to the real-life Uncas who practiced his slippery deceits against both natives and colonists in New England.

As a youthful, non-conformist clergyman in England in the 1620's, Thomas Hooker was charged with heretical opinions and was ordered to stand for trial before the High Commissioners. The outcome of any such trial at that time and place was fairly certain. So the young Mr. Hooker decided to skip rather than face the music at home. He sneaked across to Holland. Other English Puritans and Separatists had found a congenial haven in Holland and Mr. Hooker was kept occupied preaching before congregations at Amsterdam and Rotterdam.

In 1633 Mr. Hooker joined the stream of colonists crossing the ocean to America. He became pastor of the church at New Towne, or Newton (later named Cambridge).

Meanwhile, many of the colonists around Massachusetts Bay had become excited about reports of excellent farming land to the west in the valley of the Connecticut River. John Oldham of Massachusetts had made an extensive study of this area in 1633 and he brought back a highly favorable account. By this time the colonists were feeling the pinch of congestion, most of the best tillable land near the coast had been spoken for and many settlers were in a mood to pack up, head west, and try their luck in the Connecticut valley.

With Mr. Hooker as their principal clergyman, a little army of about one hundred colonists trudged west in 1635. These were the migrants who established three settlements along the river: Wethersfield, Hartford, Windsor.

In 1638 and 1639, delegates from those three little settlements met at Hartford to compose a set of laws. What emerged was a document called the Fundamental Orders, actually the world's first written constitution of a self-governing people. Mr. Hooker is conceded to have been the principal author of that historic document.

The longer state Constitution adopted later in Connecticut incorporated most of the points laid out in the Fundamental Orders. Other states in America, likewise, found that basic code in Connecticut to be a useful guide as they shaped their own Constitutions.

Mr. Hooker continued as a preacher in Hartford until his death in 1647 at the age of sixty-one.

Increase Mather

Mather was a prominent figure in both political and religious affairs in colonial New England during the latter decades of the Seventeenth Century. He was born at Dorchester, near Boston, in 1639, the son of Richard Mather who was, for many years, a minister at Dorchester.

Increase Mather graduated from Harvard, went overseas, and earned another degree at Trinity College in Dublin, Ireland, preached at churches in England and Guernsey, then returned to America and was installed as pastor of the North church in Boston. He was elected president of Harvard College in 1685 and served six years. One of his first acts upon taking over the Harvard presidency was to confer an honorary doctorate on himself.

Mr. Mather dutifully followed the strict Puritan line. He saw the evil machinations of the devil at every turn and preached a stern unyielding morality. His parishioners were warned that life was grim: "We must pass through a wilderness of miseries ere we can arrive at the heavenly Canaan." He didn't trust the pagan Indians for a moment: "Those barbarous Indians who, like their father the devil, are delighted in crueltyes." And he was sorely tried when he noticed an increase in public drunkenness, a matter which he regarded as a deliberate plot by Satan: "It is sad that ever this serpent should creep over the wilderness, where three-score years ago he never had any footing."

It was in the field of politics, however, where Mr. Mather made his most impressive mark. By 1680, certain royal circles in London had become thoroughly disenchanted with the upstart colonists in America. The King, responding to the agitation, sent an aide, Edward Randolph, to New England in 1682 to survey the situation, and Mr. Randolph began filing reports highly prejudicial to the colonial cause. Over a two-year span, Mather and Randolph engaged in lengthy and bitter disputes. In this din of controversy, Mather stoutly upheld colonial rights while Randolph maintained that the colonists had ignored royal orders and therefore didn't deserve any independent standing. The King accepted Randolph's point of view. In 1684 he forced Massachusetts Bay to surrender its charter.

For a brief period thereafter, Massachusetts was a crown colony ruled by an appointee of the King. This was an arrangement preferred by royalist leaders who never did cotton to the notion of autonomy in distant colonies.

But thanks largely to the diligent efforts of Increase Mather and a few other patriotic colonists, a favorable new charter was worked out and put into effect. It eliminated the crown colony status with the appointee of the King as governor and restored the self-government rights which the colony had enjoyed from the start. It also broadened the Massachusetts domain by merging the Plymouth colony into the new jurisdiction.

That new charter was Increase Mather's proudest accomplishment.

CONCLUSION

As the decades slipped by, descendants of the New England Puritans fanned out to other parts of America. They reached into every corner of the land - into the South, the Middle West, California, and Oregon - their stream merging with other streams of pioneers from other sections of the United States as well as from foreign lands.

After the passage of three centuries, most of the Puritans' original ideas have vanished and many of their practices have been disowned. But they left an enduring mark on our history, and millions of Americans today are proud to trace their ancestry to those Puritan settlers who braved daunting difficulties to plant their roots in America.

INDEX

Adams, Charles Francis Jr. 14
James Truslow 5 John 42 Mr.
37
An Cleeve 7
Anglican Church 3 4
Annapolis, Maryland 50
Arabella 2
Ashurst, Henry 60
Austen, Ann 45
Bale, Francis 49
Batchellor, Stephen 53
Beard, Charles A. 30 Mary R. 30
Benefit of clergy, 51
Block, Adriaen 70
Boston, Massachusetts 2 12 17 23
27 38
Bradford, William 57
Cabot, John 70 71
Calvert, Cecil 50
Calvin, John 3
Calvinism, 3 4
Cambridge, Massachusetts 27 44
49
Charles I, king of England 4
Church of England, 3
Church of Rome, 3
Clap, Roger 12 17 57
Connecticut General Court, 51 52
65
Converting the Indians, 60
Cooper, James Fenimoore 85
Cotton, John 40 52 53 64 80 81
Crossing the ocean, 5
de Brebeuf, Jean 70
de Champlain, Samuel 1 69 70
de Monts, Sieur 69
Deportation, 10
Dorchester, Massachusetts 2 12
17 20
Downing, Emmanuel 6
Drake, Francis 67

Drinker, Elizabeth 15
Dudley, Thomas 26 27
Duke of York, 74
Earl of Warwick, 83
Eddy, Mary Baker 80
Edwards, Jonathan 38
Eliot, John 83 84
Endicott, 3
Fisher, Mary 45
Franklin, Ben 31 42
Fundamental Orders, 86
Gerry, Elbridge 42
Gloucester, Massachusetts 2 23
Golden Hind 67
God's chosen remnant, 8
Gookin, Daniel 62
Gorton, Samuel 77 82 83
Hacker, Louis M. 25
Hancock, John 42
Hartford, Connecticut 13 35
Harvard College, 29
Harvard, John 29
Higginson, Francis 64 John 58
Hooker, Thomas 86
Howling wilderness, 8
Hubbard, William 62
Hudson, Henry 70 71
Hutchins, John 15
Hutchinson, Anne 77 80–83 William 80 81
Indenture system, 10 11
Indian, King Philip 61–63
Ipswich, Massachusetts 2 23
Jefferson, Thomas 42
Joan of Arc, 80
Johnson, Edward 20
Keayne, Captain 28
King Charles 78 Charles II 74
King Henry IV 69
King James 4
King Philip II 68

91

La Salle, Rene Robert Cavelier 70
Laud, William 4
Lynn, Massachusetts 2
Lyon 7
Madison, James 42
Marblehead, Massachusetts 2 21
Marquette, Jacques 70
Mary and John 12 45
Massachusetts Bay, 13 Colony 8
   20 46 57 58 64 69 78 86 87
   education 28 29 population 2
   settlement 1 smugglers 24
Massachusetts General Court, 2
   19 26–30 62 69 73 78 79 82
Mather, Cotton 29 30 63 Increase
   29 40 62 86–88 Richard 87
Mayflower 13
McPherson, Aimee Semple 80
Metacomet, 61
Miantonomo, 85
Migration, financing of 3
Minuit, Peter 71 72
Nassahegan, 65
Nation, Carrie 80
New England, Confederation 43 44
   59 Puritans 24
New Haven, Connecticut 34 50
Newbury, Massachusetts 8 15 23
   44
Newport, Rhode Island 15
Newtown Massachusetts 27
Norton, John 40
O'Leary, Mrs. 27
Oakes, Urian 40
Oldham, John 86
Pepys, Samuel 15
Phelps, Mr. 52 William 65
Philadelphia, Pennsylvania 15
Protestants, 3 4
Puritan, bigots 41 42 church–state
   theocracy 46 descendants 89
   education 30 migration to
   Massachusetts Bay in 1630's 1
   missionaries to Indians 55
   religion 33 rebels 3 Sabbath 36
   schooling 29 tolerance 54
Puritans' image of Satan 55
Puritans and adultery, 48
Puritans vs religious freedom, 40
   41
Pynchon, John 61
Queen Elizabeth, 17 67

Raleigh, Sir Walter 1
Randolph, Edward 87
Reformation, 3
Refuge for Puritan church, 5
Royal practice of granting monop-
   olies, 4
Salem, Massachusetts 2 23
   settlement 1
Saltonstall, 3
Samoset, 56
Sassacus, 84
Sehat, 65
Shakespeare, William 34
Shepard, Thomas 2 37
Sherman, Mrs. 27 28
Shipboard diet, 6
Smith, Abbott Emerson 11 John 8
Society of Friends – Quakers, 42
   43
Squanto, 57 63
Stoughton, William 60
Stuart tyranny, 5
Stuyvesant, Peter 73 75
Trade with the Indies, 22
Unbalanced populations, 8
Uncas, 84 85
United Colonies, 85
Upsall, Nicholas 45 49 58
Vane, Henry 27
Wamsutta, 61
Watertown, Massachusetts 38
Webster, Mr. 52
Williams, Roger 57 77–80 82 83
Wilson, John 38
Windsor, Connecticut 35 51 52 65
Winthrop, 4–6 27 Governor 9 13
   18 19 22 25 26 28 53 82 John 2
   8 47 64 John Jr. 7 30 31 60 75
Woodward, W. E. 79
Worcester, Massachusetts 50
Yale, 29 Elihu 30